Just As You Are

CLUB CURVE SERIES

NATALIE ARTHUR

Club Curve Series

June 2023, your favorite Contemporary Romance authors have come together to give you 30 nights you'll never forget. Every day in June you'll get to read sassy, sexy, curvy, confident women in locations all around the globe, take part in the night of their lives, at Club Curve.

<u>Just As You Are</u> is an acquaintance to lovers, hidden child, Instalove, MC romance with suspense. There is mention of characters from my Mancini Legacy and Cimaruta MC Chicago series.

✶ Created with Vellum

This is dedicated to my brother, Greg. I love you and will always miss you.

Acknowledgments

Jessica, you are summer and I am winter. Always.

Danni, this journey is so crazy! Thank you for being here with me!

JD, thank you for spending late nights with and making sure I listened even when I didn't want to. Love you.

Nicole, I'm forever grateful that you're in my life.

Carissa, thank you for everything you do.

Kristen, we can do this. Together.

Arthur, you've always supported me no matter how crazy my ideas are. I love you so much.

Mom, you've always been my biggest supporter and I don't know where I'd be without you.

Caoimhe-Lea, you drive me absolutely fucking crazy. But I wouldn't have it any other way. Love you.

Taye, and everyone I'm forgetting who has supported my crazy ideas and continue to be with me, thank you. I truly couldn't do this without all of you.

Information

No part of this book or graphics were made
with AI.
HUMAN CREATION ONLY

Just As You Are has NO cheating with a
guaranteed HEA. It is a standalone but is
connected to my Cimaruta MC Chicago Series
and my Mancini Legacy Series.

There are not a lot of dark moments or dark
issues in my books, there still are the occasions
that have to do with kidnapping, domestic abuse,
and assault.

Check out my website for current news and
trigger warnings.

Mancini Legacy and Cimaruta MC family trees.
Nataliearthurbooks.com

Mancini Legacy and Cimaruta MC Dictionary

Cage - Motorized vehicle with four wheels. (Cars)

Chicago Panthers - Professional baseball team.

Chicago Redhawks - Professional hockey team.

Cimaruta MC, Chicago - Chicago Motorcycle club, Mother charter

Cut - Vest that patched in members of the MC wear to identify who they are and their rank.

Lake Renegade Township - Town owned by the Mancini family.

Lucciola Island - 'Firefly' Island, owned by the Mancini family and located in Massachusetts.

Lucciola Memorial Hospital - Hospital in Lake Renegade Township.

Mancini Grill - 5-star restaurant located inside the Legacy Hotel.

Rockers - Top rocker has the club's name on it, the bottom rocker has the club's location.

Sprite Lake Village - Town in Illinois, owned by the Laurent family.

The Legacy Hotel - Hotel in downtown Chicago owned by the Mancini family.

Galway - Town in Ireland.

ITALIAN

Amore - Love.

Coglione - Asshole.

Colomba mia - My dove.

Cugino - Cousin.

Cuore mio - My heart.

Dolcezza - Sweetness.

Famiglia - Family.

Figlio - Son.

Fratello - Brother.

Il mio mondo - My world.

Il mio pinguino - My penguin.

Mai Andato - Never Gone.

Mi dispiace - I'm sorry.

Mi passerotta - My little sparrow.

Nonno - Grandfather.

Nonna - Grandmother.

Ti abbiamo aspettato - We waited for you.

Ti voglio bene - I love you.

Zio - Uncle.

Zia -Aunt.

<u>IRISH</u>

Aintín - Aunty

Is í Gàidhlig ár gcéad teanga - Gaelic is our first language.

Mo stór - My treasure.

<u>FRENCH</u>

D'accord petite sœur - Okay little sister

Je t'aime et Lorenzo - I love you and Lorenzo

Je t'aime - I love you

Je vous aime tous les deux - I love you both

Princesse - Princess

Toujours - Always

Toujours mes frères - Always my brothers

Tu es ma princesse - You are my princess

Cimaruta MC

President - Giacomo 'Forza' Bastianini

Vice President - Celestino 'Giustizia' Bastianini

Sgt-At-Arms - Francesco 'Bestia' Bastianini

Treasurer - Luciana 'Fuoco' Bastianini

Secretary - Isabella 'Dolce' Bastianini

Historian - Caitríona 'Forte' Bastianini

Road Captain - Connor 'Azrael' Byrne

Chaplain - Brennan 'Raziel' Doyle

Enforcer - Liam 'Amante' Murphy

Enforcer - Valentino 'Ombra' Marconi

Enforcer - Romana 'Fantasma' Vietti

Enforcer - Mitchell 'Granchio' Harris

Enforcer - Hollis 'Cavallo' Taylor

Enforcer - Rónán 'Ghiaccio' O'Callaghan

Enforcer - Fintan 'Toro' O'Callaghan

Prospect - Anthony Grimes

FAUSTO & LUNA
GRANDPARENTS
GIACOMO
SON
CAITRÍONA
DAUGHTER IN LAW
CELESTINO
GRANDSON
FRANCESCO
GRANDSON
SAOIRSE
GREAT GRANDDAUGHTER
ISABELLA
GRANDDAUGHTER
LUCIANA
GRANDDAUGHTER
GRAYSON
GREAT GRANDSON
BASTIANINI
FAMILY

KEARNEY FAMILY

Liam & Orfhlaith
GRANDPARENTS

Caitríona
DAUGHTER

Giacomo
SON IN LAW

Celestino
GRANDSON

Francesco
GRANDSON

Saoirse
GREAT GRANDDAUGHTER

Isabella
GRANDDAUGHTER

Luciana
GRANDDAUGHTER

Grayson
GREAT GRANDSON

GIACOMO
CAITRÍONA
CELESTINO
ISABELLA
FRANCESCO
LUCIANA
MAEVE
RÓNÁN
SAOIRSE
GRAYSON
BASTIANINI
FAMILY

O'CALLAGHAN

MANCINI FAMILY

Pietro & Alessia
Grandparents

Enea (T)
Son

Antonio (T)
Son

Leonardo (T)
Son

Gráinne
Daughter-in-law

Rosaura
Daughter-in-law

Sebastiano*
Grandson

Salvatore^
Grandson

Domenico*
Grandson

Fiorella^
Granddaughter

Lorenzo+
Grandson

Gianluca^
Grandson

Giovanna+
Granddaughter

Rowan
Great Grandson

(T) = Triplets
* = Twins
+ = Twins
^ = Triplets

MANCINI FAMILY

Contents

Just As You Are

Chapter One

Hollis

I don't think my parents are happy. They're still married, have been for twenty-seven years. But I never see them hug or kiss anymore. In fact, the last time I can remember either of them showing any affection to the other was at my baby sister's high school graduation. That was four years ago. I don't think they even sleep in the same room. I have an older brother, Simon, who's an accountant. He hasn't spoken to me since the day I became a patched member of the Cimaruta Motorcycle Club. That was five years ago. He says that he won't associate with criminals and I don't have the energy to explain to him how our MC works, so fuck him. He's always acted like he was better than me anyway because he got better grades in school and went to college, which I did not.

My baby sister, Aurora, is the only one who will talk to me. We make time to talk once a week and text as much as we can. She's an international model, and I couldn't be more proud of her.

I found my real family with the Cimaruta MC. I was seventeen when I met twin brothers, Celestino and Francesco Bastianini. I was a senior and they were juniors. Their dad is the president of the Chicago chapter of the Cimaruta MC, which is also the mother chapter. I had only known them for a few months when they invited me to one of their club barbecues. It was then that I decided I wanted to prospect for the club, if they'd let me. It took about a year, but when I was nineteen, I became a fully patched member. It's been the best six years of my life.

For the last few years, we've been changing the way we do business. We've never dealt in trafficking, but guns and drugs...well, let's just say we needed to make money somehow. But again, we've been changing the way our club operates and trying to stay on the right side of the law. The club owns real businesses now, and we even pay taxes. We own the Hawk's Nest, which is a bar. We also co-own Luminescence, a male strip club, with the Mancini family.

We even have women on our council. Caitríona 'Forte' Bastianini is our historian and the wife of our president, Giacomo 'Forza' Bastianini. After Celestino and Francesco finished prospecting, they were given their road names, 'Giustizia' and 'Bestia'. They're now on the council along with their twin sisters, Isabella 'Dolce' and Luciana 'Fuoco'. Our chapter clubs are in the process of changing their business habits to match ours. Some chapters are resisting more than others, but if they don't change their ways, they'll no longer be a part of the family. When it comes to having women on their councils, some are reluctant to follow our example, and that's okay—as long as they respect the chapters that want to change.

One by one, the Cimaruta MC council members are finding their forevers. First it was Luciana, our treasurer. Rónán is currently one of our prospects, and they got married a month ago. Next to find their forever was one of our enforcers, Liam 'Amante' Murphy. He met

Charmaine the same night I met Lila Slater. I don't think I've ever seen a more gorgeous woman, and her sense of humor matches mine perfectly. We spent the night together. The next morning I left her at the hotel because I had to meet everyone at the gym. We texted all day and she said she would call me later. But she's been avoiding me ever since. She's the first woman I've wanted to see more of, and it's driving me fucking crazy.

The other day, one of the club bunnies I used to spend time with commented that she missed me. I didn't even realize I hadn't been with her for a while. In fact, I haven't been with anyone since Lila.

I used to think that I didn't want to spend my life with just one person. Watching my parents become who they are now, why even try? I'm fairly certain they were in love at some point. I mean, they had us, and I'd like to think we came from love. But maybe not.

Lila

Growing up, my older brother, Carter,

always watched out for my sister, Diana, and me. When we were little, our parents were around to take care of us. Then one day, they were gone. Carter was sixteen, Diana was fourteen, and I was thirteen. We didn't tell anyone that they left. My dad was on disability and the checks kept coming, so we paid the bills and lived like they were still with us. Carter worked and went to school. Then when Di and I were old enough, we got jobs too. Somehow we made it work, even when I got pregnant at seventeen.

I have a daughter, Madeleine. She's five years old and the love of my life. I had her about a month after I graduated from high school. Her dad, Travis, was my world and we got married a few months after Maddie was born. He moved in with all of us because it was easier that way. We met in elementary school and were just friends for a long time. Then, when we were fourteen, things changed. We were at the lake just hanging out, and he kissed me. I'd had a crush on him for so long, and when he finally took that step, I was in heaven. From that moment on? Every minute we could spend together, we did. We pushed each other to do well in school. Even after I got pregnant, Travis said we needed to finish so that we could provide our baby with the best life possible. So that's what we did. We got married, then Travis went to college to become a certified mechanic. He did everything he could to support the three of us because he didn't want our baby to go to day care unless it was absolutely necessary.

We had a great life right up until he left us. I still don't know what happened—I never saw it coming. The only thing I do know is that there was another woman. That was three years ago, and it was the worst day of my life. I felt like I didn't even know how to breathe after he left. But I knew I had to keep going for my daughter. I was lucky, my brother and sister stepped up and both help me as much as they can.

I have two jobs—one I love, and one I keep because I need the money. The job I love is being a server at the Mancini Grill, which is located inside the Legacy hotel. I started working there about six months before Travis left, and I've been waiting for a bartending position to open up. When it does become available, management has promised me it's mine. Two months ago I started working at Club Curve—I'm a bartender there. The real money is in stripping, but I just can't get myself to do it. My coworkers are nice, but the clientele can be iffy sometimes. I've seen dancers have problems with some of the guys that come in. They hit on the bartenders too, of course. These guys think we owe them something because they tip us for drinks. It's funny because some are pretty shitty tippers. I'm not going home with anyone, especially not when they tip me like two dollars on a fifty dollar tab. Also, leaving me a phone number doesn't pay my bills.

When I was in school I never had any close friends. I basically only had my brother, my sister and Travis. I met my current besties when I started working at the Mancini Grill. They're part of my family now. There are five of us: Chloe, Faith, Charmaine, and Charmaine's sister, Violet. They've really helped me through the last three years. I've always had a hard time asking anyone for anything, but they've taught me that it's okay to need help. I still struggle, but my girls and my siblings make it a little easier.

Chapter Two

Hollis

I'm not sure why Lila ghosted me. Okay, she hasn't really ghosted me, I see her when she comes to the clubhouse with Charmaine, but she doesn't come over and talk to me. As much as I want to chase her, I don't know if that's what she wants. Now, I'm not the kind of guy that falls at women's feet. But there's something about Lila that makes me want her in my life, even if we're just friends. Nah, fuck that. I want her with me. And not as a friend.

The night we met, we had such a good time. I was surprised when she agreed to go home with me. But I'm so damn glad she did, because being with her was better than it was with anyone I've been with before. Then we spent the morning together, and texted throughout the day. But the next day? Crickets.

I could probably get Amante to ask Charmaine. Or hell, I can just ask Charmaine myself. But that'll make me look like a pussy. Besides, we're not in high school, I can work without a net. It's driving me fucking crazy because I can't stop thinking about her.

It's Friday night and my club brothers and I are sitting around at the clubhouse. We had church earlier, and after that we usually go to the Hawk's Nest.

"We need to get out. Any ideas?" Mitchell 'Granchio' Harris, one of our enforcers, asks.

"Why not just go to the Hawk's Nest?" Romano 'Fantasma' Vietti laughs.

"I was just thinking maybe we could try somewhere new." Granchio sighs.

"What about Club Curve? I've driven by it before, we all have. But I never thought to go in. If you want something new, let's try there," our road captain, Connor 'Azrael' Byrne responds.

"Dance club? Or strip club?" Fantasma asks.

Azrael shrugs his shoulders and chuckles. "Does it matter? Worth going in to find out."

Everyone agrees, so we all get on our bikes and head to Club Curve.

Lila

It's hard to believe that it's been two months since I met a man who I just can't stop thinking about. His name is Hollis 'Cavallo' Taylor. After Travis left us, I didn't think I would ever meet someone that made me feel the way he did. But meeting Hollis brought back all those butterfly feelings. And it scares the shit out of me because I like him so much in such a short time.

The night we met was a rare night out with my girls: Faith, Charmaine, Violet and Chloe. Our days off usually never match up. Plus, I hate to ask Diana or Carter to watch Maddie, even though I know they would. We had decided to go to a bar called the Hawk's Nest, which we later found out is owned by the Cimaruta Motorcycle Club. Charmaine's ex followed us there and started shit with her. He's a creeper who wouldn't leave her alone even though they'd broken up almost a year ago. She ended up being rescued by a sexy, muscled, heavily-tattooed biker named Liam 'Amante' Murphy. It's been two months since that night. They're engaged now, and I couldn't be happier for my bestie.

My girls have all been saying that I'm crazy for keeping Hollis at arm's length. Especially Charmy, she's always telling me that if I keep doing this, I might miss out on the love of my life. Love. Psh. She's still in her little love bubble and wants all of us to be in one too. I loved Travis with all my heart and look what happened. Just cause she was lucky enough to find her forever with Amante doesn't mean I'm going to find mine with Hollis.

The night I met Hollis, I got caught up in the excitement and made the mistake of going home with him. I only say it was a mistake because I've never gone home with anyone the same night I met them. But even after we spent the night together, I didn't have the urge to run away. That's a new feeling for me. Hollis said he wants to be with me. But I just don't know.

I haven't told him about my Maddie. I had one relationship after Travis left, and the guy screwed me over. It was about a year after Travis had gone. Maddie was around three years old at the time. His name was Adam, and he was sexy as hell. After a month of dating, I decided to introduce him to Maddie, and he seemed to adore her. I even trusted him to watch her a few times when I worked an afternoon or evening shift. Then one night when Maddie and I were just hanging out, she started talking about other women. Women I didn't know. So I asked her who they were, and she said that they were Adam's friends. They would go to the mall and meet up with them. They even played a game where she called him 'Daddy'. I was just about to call Adam and tell him to fuck off. But Chloe called me first and said she saw him at the mall where he was walking with some girl. They were holding hands. Chloe, being my bestie, followed them. After a couple of hours, they parted ways, but not before hugging and kissing. After Adam left, she confronted the girl. She told Chloe that she had just started seeing Adam—a single father. That asshole was using my little girl to pick up other women.

So after that? I avoided relationships like the plague. I've been out with guys—dinner, maybe a movie, but never anything serious. Sometimes I just want someone to spend a little time with. And I'm upfront about that from the start. I don't want them to think it's going to last forever. There have been a few that I've slept with, but again, they knew upfront that I wasn't looking for a relationship. More like a friends-with-benefits thing.

Maddie was so little when Travis left us that she doesn't really remember him. As angry as I still am about what he did, I won't be the kind of mom that tells her kid their dad's an asshole. One day she'll figure that out for herself.

Most nights working at Club Curve go pretty smooth. Tonight we have two bachelor parties, and everyone's behaving themselves so far. But there's an obnoxious asshole here somewhere, I just know it.

"How much for you to come over here and entertain us?" a guy says to my back, right on cue. I sigh and slowly turn around to see three guys leering at me.

"Sorry, I'm just here to serve drinks. If you want something specific for your party, you need to talk to Janet. She's the one at the end of the bar," I say to them.

"I wanna see what *you* can do. So how much, sweetheart?"

Alrighty then. Looks like tonight we're dealing with the Thick-Headed Asshole, not an uncommon breed around here. What usually works is just ignoring them. Most are here to get drunk and have fun—I like the guys who respect boundaries. No one is allowed to touch the dancers or the bartenders, and security makes sure of that.

One of the guys I'm ignoring whistles at me. It's piercing, like he thinks we're at a fucking ballgame or something. Next thing that happens is him being escorted out the door. No one tries to defend him, which makes me chuckle. Most of the time, the friends don't help. The other two leave me alone after their buddy gets kicked out, which makes me happy. I'm really not in the mood tonight.

Chapter Three

Hollis

From the outside, it looks like any other dance club. There's a short line to get in, made up of mostly men. We have Fuoco, Dolce and Charmaine with us tonight. Some of the guys in line have made inappropriate comments to them and it didn't go over well. Those guys will be partying somewhere else tonight.

We pay the cover charge and go in. I'm not sure what I expected to see, but it's a classy setup. Not like some of the other strip clubs we've been to. There's a few girls dancing in cages suspended from the ceiling and one up on stage. There's also a regular dance floor. None of the dancers are naked, but they're still captivating. And now I'm imagining Lila in a cage like that dancing only for me. Holy fuck, now I'm hard. That woman makes me crazy.

There's a commotion at the bar—a guy is reaching over it, trying to grab the bartender. Wait. That's my Lila. Oh fuck no. I rush to the bar and grab the fucker that's touching my girl. After I pull him back, my brothers take him from me so I can tend to Lila.

I put my hand out to help her up.

___

Lila

___

"Hey baby, how much for a dance?"

And here we go again. I roll my eyes and take a deep breath, letting it out slowly. Tonight has gotten worse after that first guy got tossed out. This guy is here with one of the bachelor parties as well, and it's been non-stop drunken pick-up lines. Most of them are being shouted at the dancers, but some are directed at me.

"Look, I told your buddies earlier—I make drinks, I don't dance." I turn to reach for a vodka bottle. Next thing I know, someone's got the kung fu grip on my ponytail and my head is jerked roughly back. Off balance, I hit the ground. As I'm getting up to tell this asshole off, he's being pulled away from the bar. I thought it was our bouncer, Matt, but I hear a different, familiar voice. One that I never wanted to hear in here. Hollis. Dammit.

"Are you okay, Lila?" Hollis asks as he puts his hand out to help me up.

"Yeah, thanks. Wh-what are you doing here?" My hand is shaking as I take hold of his.

"The boys wanted to try somewhere new. I didn't know you worked here. I thought you worked at the Mancini Grill?"

I snatch my hand back. "Look, I don't need you judging me for working here. And it's none of your fucking business what I do anyway."

"Whoa, cupcake. Back up. No one's judging you. Do I like that you work in a place where men can touch you? Fuck no. But I would never judge you for the choices you make."

Well now I feel like an ass. The look in Hollis' eyes is the same one he gave me the night we met, like I was the only woman in the room. I've tried to keep my distance—I don't want a relationship. Every once in a while I meet someone and we have some fun, but I make sure to keep it casual. No feelings. Plus, with Maddie, I don't have a lot of time to myself.

"No one touches me. Usually. That guy was just a dick. And don't call me 'cupcake'. I'm not food," I grumble.

"You're delicious," he whispers in my ear as he takes my hand.

It sends shivers down my body. Fuck. I look up at him and he's smiling at me. Okay fine. I'm a little insecure about my appearance. I'm not a walking twig, I'm a fluffy branch. And with the way the dancers are eyeing him and his club brothers? Yeah. They could have their pick. Yet his gaze is fixed on me.

"Stop staring at me," I snap. "And let me go, I gotta get back to work."

"What if I don't want to let you go, Lila? You said you would call, but you ghosted me. And I'm not going to let you do that again," he says quietly to me.

I frown at him. "I didn't ghost you. I've just been busy. As you can see, I have two jobs. I don't have a whole lot of free time." I don't know why I'm throwing so much attitude his way. He's the last person that deserves it. But I can't help being defensive.

"Why are you mad at me? Every time I see you at the clubhouse, I try to talk to you, but you disappear."

He does sound disappointed that I keep running from him.

"Okay, if you want me to stop chasing you, you need to say it, cupcake. Otherwise I *will* make sure you know how much I want you."

Wait. What is even happening? He keeps saying he wants me and I don't know what to do with that.

"Do you want me to back off, cupcake?"

I slowly shake my head no.

"Good. That's the answer I was looking for. What time do you get off tonight?"

"Um. We do last call at two-fifteen, close at three. I'm usually out pretty close to that."

He nods at me. "Did you drive to work?"

"I did."

"Give me your keys. I'll have Granchio take your car to the clubhouse. You can ride with me when you're done."

"I'm not getting on your bike when you've been drinking." I may have a haze of lust surrounding me when it comes to Hollis, but that doesn't mean I'll ride with him if he's buzzed.

"Cupcake, I haven't touched any alcohol tonight, so if that's your only rule, I'm down."

I must be hallucinating. Maybe I bumped my head. Because why else would Hollis be chasing me and agreeing to whatever I say?

In a daze, I start to turn so I can get back to work when he grabs me from across the bar and kisses me. Not just an oh-hello kiss. It's a you're-mine-and-everyone-here-is-going-to-know-it kiss. I melt into him as I feel his tongue running across my lips. I moan and kiss him back.

His club brothers are whistling at us, and as I break the kiss, I can feel the heat rising on my cheeks.

"I still need your keys, Lila."

"Let me get some drinks out, and I'll get them. They're in my locker," I say to him.

He nods and takes a seat at the bar. I watch him scan the room and scowl at any guy who looks in my direction. As soon as I get caught up with drinks, I slip back to the locker room, grab my keys and bring them out to him.

———————————————

Hollis

"That's my girl," I say as Lila hands me her keys.

"Can you get Lila's car to the clubhouse for me?" I ask Granchio.

"We can do that," Charmaine says. I see her wink at Lila. Lila responds by sticking her tongue out at her.

"Are you sure?" I say.

"Definitely. We were gonna leave in a bit anyway."

I hand the keys to Charmaine and thank her. I give her some time with Lila while I look around the club. I've been noticing some of the assholes in here staring at my girl. Fuck that. If she insists on working here, I'm gonna plant my ass on this barstool for every minute of every shift. I don't even care if her boss doesn't like it. Maybe I should see about having her bartend at Luminescence or the Hawk's Nest. At least I know she'll be safe at those places.

I'm still wondering why she works here. It doesn't feel like the kind of place my cupcake would choose to work, with all these assholes constantly hitting on her. And what would've happened if we weren't here when that prick basically assaulted her? The bouncer was too far away. By the time he could have gotten there, that fucker would've been on her. My anger is bubbling again as I think about it.

After saying bye to Amante and Charmaine, I continue to watch Lila. She does her best to ignore the drunk fuckers at the bar—she's had to cut off a few. The bouncer, who I found out is named Matt, calls them a cab and gets them out. But I still don't like it. Tonight is going to be her last night at Club Curve.

"Thank you," I say to Lila as she refills my soda.

"Why are you just sitting here? There's other things to do here at the club, you know." She's looking at me funny.

"Like what?" I frown.

"Do you not see the girls dancing? There's private shows too, and I know some of the girls will do extras for certain clients."

The look on my girl's face is killing me. "Lila, there's only one woman I want a show from and she's standing in front of me serving drinks."

She squints at me, like she thinks I'm lying. But I don't care—if I have to spend every waking moment showing her what I see when I look at her? Then that's what I'm going to do.

"Why do you work here?" I ask her.

She shrugs her shoulders. "I make good money here."

My eyes narrow. "How many nights do you work?"

She squints at me again. "Just Fridays and Saturdays. Why?"

Oh fuck no. "You should give your notice tonight. Or better yet, this can be your last shift."

"Whoa, back the fuck up. I need to work. I have bills and responsibilities. I can't just stop working. I make more here than at the Grill," she snaps. "And I'm not quitting there either."

Bills I can handle. Not that she'd let me pay them, but I could. "How about I get you a job at one of the places the club owns? There's the Hawk's Nest and Luminescence."

She perks up when I mention Luminescence. Ugh. Of course she'd want the strip club. But I work there too, so it's the perfect arrangement.

"Luminescence? Could you get me both nights there?"

She's beaming. Fuck me. "Yes, cupcake. I can get you both. I know you've been to the shows, so you've probably seen we have three bartenders on each night and a few servers too. You want to bartend?"

"Yes. Please."

"Will you quit this place tonight?"

"If you promise I can start tomorrow? Yes."

I nod. "Let me go talk to Giustizia. I'll be right back."

Chapter Four

Hollis

She's still smiling as I walk over to Giustizia. I know he'll say yes, but I can't just do this without his okay.

"Your girl's got some spunk." Granchio laughs.

I roll my eyes at him. "Don't I know it. Hey Giustizia, I have a question for you."

"Sure, what's up?" he responds.

"I want Lila to quit working here. The only way she'll do that is if I can get her a job at Luminescence, Friday and Saturday nights bartending." I stare at him as he starts to laugh.

"Holy shit. You've known this woman for what? Two months? You haven't even gone out with her and you've claimed her?"

And here it comes. I love my club brothers, but they can—and will—make fun of anything. Especially when one of us finds our forever. They're still giving Amante shit about being a 'kept' man.

"Bring it on. Let's have it." I laugh at them.

They all start laughing and ribbing me about Lila.

"Seriously though, of course she can have one of the positions. In fact, it's great timing. Ester just told me she has a family emergency back home in Spain and had to leave this morning," Giustizia says.

"I hope everything's okay. But the timing is perfect. Thanks, brother."

He smiles and slaps me on the back. "Go get your girl."

I can't help smiling as I walk back to Lila. I wait for her to finish serving the guys sitting at the bar. Then I motion for her to come over to me.

"The shifts are yours. Fridays and Saturdays at Luminescence. You start tomorrow. They're long nights, but there's three of you. Start times are staggered. First at four, second at six and third at eight," I explain to her.

"Holy shit, you did it? Okay so wait, do all three stay and close?"

"The first one on leaves around midnight. Second leaves at closing. Third does the final clean up and gets off around three. You can take whichever shift you want."

"Can I ask which shift makes the most?"

I chuckle. "Sure. Generally, the mid shift or closer makes the most. That's because the first shift goes home before the night is over."

"Hmm. That makes sense. Can I get the closing shift?" she asks.

"Definitely. I'll text the other two bartenders and let them know."

I text Marshall and Angelo. They not only bartend for us, they started prospecting about three months ago. So I know Lila will be safe with them.

Cavallo: Got a new bartender starting tomorrow

Angelo: What happened to Ester?

Cavallo: Family emergency. She's back in Spain

Marshall: That sucks. Who's the newbie?

Cavallo: Her name is Lila. Look out for her. She's my girl and we all know how some of the customers can get. She wants the closing shift. So you two work out the opening and mid

Marshall: Got it. You don't have to worry. You working too?

Cavallo: Of course. Every Friday and Saturday from now on

Angelo: LOL. I'll take mid if that's cool

Marshall: Sounds good to me. I'll be in at 4

Cavallo: Works for me. See you guys tomorrow

"Okay, it's all set up, cupcake. You start at eight tomorrow night. I'll pick you up if that's okay."

Lila

"Nah, I can drive myself. I have some things I need to get done before work," I say.

"It wasn't really a question," he says. It feels like he's studying me. "I want to know you, everything about you. It seems like you're afraid of something and I know it'll take time, but you can trust me."

I don't know how to respond to that. What if he leaves when I tell him about Maddie? Not a lot of men want to take care of a child that's not theirs. When Travis left, I did hope that maybe one day I'd find someone to love the two of us again.

But after Adam, I didn't introduce Maddie to anyone else. I was lucky all he did was pretend to be her daddy. What if the next one touched her? I could never live with that. I'll kill anyone that touches my baby.

So as much as I like Hollis and feel like maybe he's different, I just don't know. My girls tell me that I don't have to be so paranoid. He's a good man, and it's not like he'll be babysitting Maddie by himself anytime soon. And I know that. But I don't want Maddie to get attached. When I broke up with Adam, she spent months asking what she did wrong and if he was going to come back. I don't want her to go through that again. And if it means I'll be single till she leaves for college? Then that's what I'll do.

"You don't have to pick me up and take me to work to get to know me."

"True, cupcake. But let me tell you something—I've never wanted to take it past a night of fun before. You make me want to know you. I want to spend time with you, even if it's just driving to work."

"Getting to know me might make you turn tail and run."

Hollis

Why would she say that? What happened to my girl to make her think she's not worth it? She's beautiful. Every curve she has makes me want to run my hands all over them. And for once, it's not just a sexual attraction for me. I want to know her. What makes her smile. What her dreams are. Thank god my club brothers can't hear what's going on in my head. It feels like she's hiding something, though. There's a sadness in her eyes even when she's smiling. I'm tempted to text Charmaine and ask her. But I think this is something Lila needs to tell me herself. So I'm going to try and be as patient as I can.

"So what do you say?"

At this point I'm practically begging her.

"Maybe. Let me see if I can get my shit together."

"Okay, cupcake." I lean over the bar and kiss her. That gets me a smile. Who knew a simple smile could make you feel like you won the lottery?

I take a look around. The bachelor parties are getting rowdier. I'm glad we're here so they can't mess with my girl. A few guys have tried, but all it's taken is a look from me or one of my brothers to make them stop.

It's finally last call and apparently the drunk asses don't like it. Well tough shit. It looks like Matt the bouncer might need some help getting the bachelor parties out of here.

I've watched Lila work all night and I admire the way she handles the guys at the bar. I can see that she's tough but fair, and she doesn't take shit from any of them.

The manager on duty, Janet, lets us stay after we help get all the other patrons out. I wait with my brothers for Lila to finish talking to Janet about quitting. I know it's shitty to ask Lila to quit with no notice and leave them hanging. If they really need a temporary bartender, I'm sure we can help them. I refuse to have her working here another night.

"Okay, I'm ready to go," Lila says as she walks up to me.

"Everything okay?" I ask as I take her hand.

"Yeah, Janet said she was surprised I lasted this long." She laughs.

I laugh with her as I pull her closer to me. "Thank you for doing this. I don't like that you had to work here."

She looks down, and now I know there's a reason for it.

"What made you stay? Are you okay?" I ask.

"I-I'm fine. I just have bills. And this was the best way for me to make the money I need."

"If it's the money, I can give you money."

"NO!" She gasps. "I mean no, thank you. I appreciate the gesture, but I can do this."

"I didn't mean it like you couldn't, I just want to help you."

I wish she would open up to me. Maybe she doesn't feel what I do? And when did I start having feelings? What the fuck is going on?

"Look, I appreciate that you want to help me. But I don't need a handout."

I take a deep breath. She's not going to make this easy. So I stay quiet and put my arm around her shoulders.

"Let's get going." When we get to my bike, I pull out the helmet I bought for her.

"You just carry an extra helmet around?"

"Cupcake, I've never had anyone on the back of my bike. I got that helmet for you right after we met."

Chapter Five

Lila

Wait, did he just say he bought it for me? Why would he do that? Half of me is insisting that I see where this goes with Hollis. But the other half is saying he'll meet Maddie, get scared and bolt. Maybe I should just tell him about her now and see what he says. Better to rip the band-aid off sooner than later, before I get more attached.

I take the helmet and put it on. Then I get on the bike behind Hollis and wrap my arms around him. I can tell he's taking the long way to the clubhouse, and I can't say I object. I love being on his bike with him. It feels like I'm flying as I breathe in the night air. It's like nothing I've ever experienced before.

Knowing that I'm the first woman to ever be on his bike makes me feel oddly possessive of him. Add to that the rumble of the bike under my ass? I want to jump him right here, right now. But I have to keep my head on straight—telling him about Maddie is my first priority.

We pull into the driveway at the clubhouse and we're greeted by one of the new prospects. I remember meeting him last week. No one is allowed through the gates unless they know you. The Cimaruta MC has a lot of strict rules about who is allowed onto the property. I've heard they've had issues with other clubs. But I'm not really in the 'inner circle' so I don't know any details.

I do know that ever since Charmaine and Amante have been together, the club has become an important part of her life. I love how happy she's been since meeting him. I want that—what Charmaine and Amante have. We'll see what happens after I tell Hollis about my Maddie. Will he run?

"What's going on in that gorgeous head of yours?" Hollis asks.

I didn't realize I'd been daydreaming. I look

up at him. He's so damn handsome, with his baby-blue eyes and wavy, dark-brown hair. Muscles and tattoos in all the right places. I see the way women look at him, and I wonder what he sees in me. I'm not exactly rocking the skinny model look.

"I need to tell you something and I'm not sure how you're going to react to it." I can't keep the nervousness out of my voice as he studies my face.

"You can tell me anything."

Hollis

As long as she doesn't tell me that she's married or with someone, I'm pretty sure I can handle anything else she has to say. She looks really nervous.

"I-I have a daughter. I don't tell most people about her because it's not easy to date as a single mom."

Holy shit. That's her big secret?

I smile at her. "What's her name? How old is she?"

I watch her eyes get bigger as she looks at me.

I don't know why she thought she couldn't tell me.

"She's five years old and her name is Madeleine. I call her Maddie."

"When can I meet her? I understand if it's too soon," I blurt out.

She pulls her phone out and shows me a picture of the most adorable little girl. She has Lila's caramel-brown eyes and almost-black hair.

"She's beautiful, just like her mama."

I finally get a smile from Lila. "Is Maddie the reason you're working two jobs?"

"She's part of the reason. I hate being away from her, but I want her to have everything she needs."

"I hope I'm not overstepping, but where's her father?" Lila looks down and I hear her take a sharp breath like she's trying not to cry. I reach for her and wrap my arms around her. "I'm sorry I asked. Please don't cry, baby."

She sniffles. "It's okay. Travis left us about three years ago. I found out a few months later that he cheated on me. I'm not sure how long it had gone on, or if he left me for the girl he cheated with. But I haven't heard from him since, so I can't ask him."

Dammit. Now I have to kill him for hurting

my girls. Fucking deadbeat dad. They're some of the worst fuckers walking this earth.

"I'm so sorry, cupcake," I say as I hold her tighter. "Who is our Maddie with when you're at work?"

"When I worked at the club, she stayed overnight with my sister or my brother. We live in a triplex, so we each have our own area. When I work at the Grill, they just watch her till I'm done and then I pick her up."

"So we pick her up in the morning?"

"I usually get her after lunch. They don't mind unless they have something to do."

I nod. "We can go get her now if you want."

"Do you live here in the clubhouse?" she asks.

"No, I have a house on the property. All of us do. We usually only use our clubhouse rooms when we drink too much. It's easier than trying to stumble our way home."

She giggles and finally wraps her arms around me. I kiss the top of her head. I'm definitely not gonna let her go now.

"It's late. I can get her later today. I'm sure they're all sleeping."

"Okay, let's go inside. I'm sure everyone's still

up." I take her hand and we walk into the clubhouse together.

Lila

Charmaine comes running up to me and hugs me.

"I'm so glad you're here. Luciana went to bed early, but Isabella stayed up with me." She laughs. "Are you and Cavallo together now?" she adds quietly.

"I just told him about Maddie. I figured he should know now. Because if he's going to run, I want him to run now and not later."

"I told you he wouldn't. And judging by the look he's giving you? I don't think there's really anything you could say that would make him run." She chuckles.

As I'm looking around, I see a few women dressed in almost nothing. Some are sitting on the guys' laps and some are grinding on them. The few times I've been here, they've been dressed and weren't trying to have sex in public.

"Don't worry about them. Some are bitches but for the most part, once it's said that Cavallo is taken, they'll leave him alone," Charmaine says softly. It's like she can read my mind.

"Why would I be worried? I'm not even sure if we're a thing yet. Besides, it's kind of fast for me to be claiming him. He's free to do whatever and whoever he wants."

"You're full of shit, Li. I know you better than that, so don't bullshit me."

I sigh. "Fine. Of course I don't want him fucking them. But what if he doesn't want anything serious? This could be just a way to pass the time for him."

Charmaine makes me look straight at her. "If there's one thing I know about the men of this club? When they find their person, they're done. There's no playing around, no wondering if they're in or out. They're all in. You've seen Luciana and Rónán, Isabella and Finn too. With Giacomo and Caitríona, you can see the love between them."

Everything she's saying is great. But that doesn't mean Hollis and I will be like them. Do I want it? Hell yes. But I don't think I'll ever get it. As I'm starting to feel sorry for myself, I feel arms circling my waist. Instinctively I know it's Hollis, I don't know how. But when he touches me, calmness washes over me.

"Will you spend the night with me?" he whispers in my ear.

I turn so that I can look into his eyes, but he doesn't loosen his grip.

"Yes."

One simple little word and his face lights up with the biggest smile. I can't help but smile back at him.

"I'm going to show you what you mean to me," he adds.

I shiver slightly at his words. They bring back memories of the night we spent together. It was the best sex I've ever had, and now all I can think about is his cock. I'm so screwed.

"You ready to go to bed?" Hollis asks me just as I yawn.

I chuckle. "Yeah, bed sounds good."

"You know you won't be sleeping just yet."

Yep. It's going to be a sleepless night. Not that I'm complaining.

"Are we going to your house?" I ask as I follow him.

"That's up to you, cupcake."

"I'd like to see your house. But I have a question."

"You can ask me anything, baby. Nothing's off-limits."

I take a deep breath. "Have you had women in your bed at your house?"

He shakes his head no. "You would be the first. I won't lie, I've had women here at the clubhouse. But mostly we went to a hotel. The club doesn't like having strangers on the property."

"So wait. You've been with some of these women that are here right now?" I'm trying not to sound jealous. But I am. I hate the idea that he's touched these women.

He has a weird look on his face. "Do you really wanna know? You don't have to worry about the bunnies here."

"I do want to know. What are bunnies?" Charmaine already told me about the bunnies. But I have to play dumb because I'm not sure if it was okay for her to tell me or not. They used to be called 'sweetbutts'. But when Luciana and Isabella were teenagers, they said those women bounce around between the brothers like rabbits. So from then on, they've been called bunnies. "And how long has it been since you've been with these 'bunnies'?"

These are answers I'm not so sure I want to know. But I feel like I need to know. Since we got here, I've noticed one bunny that won't stop glaring at me. I'm guessing she's one of them.

"The last one was Alice, she's the one staring at us. The last time I was with her was a few weeks before we met. I haven't been with anyone else since you."

Could he really be telling me the truth? I want to believe him and let him in. But I don't know if I can. And right on cue, she comes walking over. She's wearing booty shorts, of course, and a sports bra, if you can call it that.

Chapter Six

Hollis

I can see the doubt in my girl's eyes and I don't like it. And because Alice wants to be a bitch, she comes over to start something. I told her the week I met Lila that we wouldn't be hanging out anymore. She didn't take it well, but because she hasn't bothered me since then, I thought she would respect my boundaries. Apparently not.

"Hey lover, time for bed?" She tries to lean in and nip my ear. I pull back and stare at her.

"Not with you, Alice. I told you the deal and if you don't step off, you're outta here."

She snorts at me. "You'll come crawling back

to me. I know what you like, and this bitch can't give you that."

I nod at our newest prospect and he heads over to us.

"Get her out," I tell him. He nods at me and tries to escort her outside.

"Fuck you, Cavallo! You had your cock in me last night and now you want to act like this?" she screams. "This bitch waltzes in and you just fall at her feet like the pussy you are. You may have a big dick, but you don't know how to fucking use it."

I laugh at her outburst because it's sealed her fate. She'll never be allowed back on this property or any property the MC owns. Bunnies don't get to yell at patched members or their women. No matter what.

A few weeks before I met Lila, it started to feel like Alice wanted more. I never have, and I made that clear from the beginning. She agreed and said she understood. Plus, I knew she was still fucking some of my club brothers. Which isn't a big deal, we all know what's going on with the bunnies. Unless one of the brothers claims her? Well then, it's anyone's game.

The other bunnies are watching. Some are glaring at Lila, and some are smirking at Alice.

They're all out for themselves. Some of my brothers like them, so they'll be allowed to hang around until no one has any need for them. But the one thing they do know is to stay out of shit like this. Especially if they want to stay.

We need to check the bunnies out more thoroughly. I don't have the time or patience for this. And the look in my Lila's eyes tells me that Alice mouthed off enough to put doubt in her mind. Fuck.

Giacomo 'Forza' Bastianini, the president of our club, comes walking into the clubhouse.

"What in the fuck is going on?" he growls.

"Forza! Thank god you're here. Cavallo made me promises—he made me his woman last week and now he's acting like I'm just a common whore." Alice sobs.

I hear Fuoco snicker. "You *are* a common whore. If I remember correctly, you went to Forza this morning and tried to tell him the same story about Rónán. That he was leaving me and wanted you instead." She laughs even more. "And because you're not only a common whore, but a lying whore, you were kicked off the property. Now I don't know how the fuck you weaseled your way back in, but if I see you here again or anywhere you're not supposed to be? You're going to have problems. Serious fucking problems. Prospect, get her the fuck out, find out who let her in, and bring him to me."

"Got it, Fuoco," he says as he drags Alice out screaming.

"What in the fuck is going on?" roars Giustizia, as he passes them on his way in. "You can hear that bitch clear as hell outside."

I sigh. "Lila and I were just heading out, and Alice started this shit."

"I had her banned this morning—and I was going to mention it at church tonight. But since most of us are here—if any of you see her on this property, in the bar, or in the club? Make sure she's kicked out and call Salvatore Mancini. He's been made aware that she's banned," Forza says.

Everyone acknowledges that they heard him loud and clear. This night has turned into a huge shit storm and I'm fucking over it.

"Are you ready to go?" I ask Lila.

She looks up at me. "I think I should head home."

Fuck me. This is what I was afraid of. "Let me take you home. It's late, and I don't want you driving."

"I'm fine to drive." She frowns.

"Cupcake, you have two choices. Either stay

at my place or I drive you home. There's no third option."

I'm not going to let her run away from me again. I know pushing her too much too fast probably isn't the right thing to do either. But I can't lose her now. Especially after what Alice said.

"Fine. I'll stay at your place. But I'm sleeping on the couch."

"No. You'll sleep in my bed, and I'll take the couch."

She rolls her eyes at me. "You're a stubborn ass."

I laugh.

Lila

Hollis' house isn't anything like I imagined it would be. It's a two-story, craftsman-style house, and it's beautiful. There's a wrap-around porch with chairs and a table. I follow him inside and am speechless at what he's created. In his living room is a couch and a TV, with a see-through fireplace connecting to his library. There's floor to ceiling built-in bookshelves. About half are filled with books.

"It's a work in progress," he says as I take it all in.

"It's beautiful. I could live in this room."

"You're welcome to come over and read anything you want. And you can add to it if you like."

His voice does things to me that it shouldn't, especially after hearing Alice's tirade. I don't know what to think. I don't want to doubt Hollis because of a bitch like her. But he did admit he's been with her. And probably more than once. That makes my stomach turn. The thought of his hands on her...the same hands I love on me. That perfect mouth on her body. Fuck, I need to stop or I'm going to drive myself crazy.

"I know what you're thinking, cupcake," he whispers in my ear. "No woman has been in here. Well, just my sister, and the women in the club. But they don't count."

I turn and face him. "I keep imagining you with Alice. I'm sorry, but I can't get it out of my head."

Hollis wraps his arms around me. "I wish I could take all of it back. But you should know it was never anything serious. I never wanted to be with just one woman before. Then I met you, and everything changed. Growing up, I didn't have the best role models. My family is fucked up, and the only one I talk to anymore is my baby sister, Aurora. But you make me look at things differently. You're the first and last woman that will ever be on the back of my bike and in my bed."

"What if I can't give you what you want?" Truthfully, I'm afraid I'm not enough for him. "I mean let's be realistic, Hollis. Look at me. I'm not exactly the kind of girl that you usually hang out with. You attract stunning women. I've seen you at the clubhouse. Women are attracted to you like moths to a flame."

"You've been watching me?" He grins at me.

I shake my head. "That's what you got out of my little speech?"

"Yep." He's still grinning at me. "You are the most beautiful woman I've ever seen. And since I've been lucky enough to have you? I know I don't want to let you go. I can't force you to be with me. But I don't want you to ever doubt yourself because of me. And in case you're not getting what I'm saying—I want you, Lila. Only you."

I don't know what to say to him. Now I'm not

usually insecure about the way I look. But the bunnies that hang around the club? Yeah, they bring it out in me. And I don't like it.

"You remember I have a daughter, right? I can't just leave her with my brother or sister and hang out here all the time."

"I don't expect you to do that. In fact, I wish you could be okay with bringing her here."

"Bring Maddie here? There's no other kids for her to play with."

"My club brothers are like big kids. She'd have a lot of fun here," he says.

"Why don't we start with you meeting her first."

I can't believe I'm saying he should meet Maddie. What the fuck is wrong with me? I've never introduced Maddie to someone this fast. In fact, Adam's the only one she ever met. And well, look how that turned out.

Something is telling me that Hollis wouldn't do that to me or Maddie. But sometimes fear wins over courage.

"We can take this slow if you want. But I want you to know I'm all in. I'm not going anywhere. You're it for me and if you're not on the same page yet, I'll wait for you to catch up."

"I want to be on the same page as you. But I'm just not there yet. I'm sorry."

"Don't be sorry, baby. We'll figure us out."

He wraps his huge body around me and I feel so safe. Maybe we will get there.

Chapter Seven

Hollis

It's been a couple of weeks since the incident with Alice, and things have been going well with Lila and me. She isn't ready to introduce me to Maddie yet. But we talk every day. And she's been letting me pick her up for her shifts at Luminescence. So that's a step in the right direction. This weekend is one of our club barbecues. We have them once a month and Luminescence is closed for the whole weekend. This barbecue is one we're having before the Bastianini family goes to Ireland. It's a big weekend for their family, and they wanted to have the barbecue before they left.

I know Lila's worried about the money she's losing out on this weekend. I offered to help her if she needs it. She's gotten a little better at letting me do things for her. Like this week, I got her some groceries. I had them delivered so I wouldn't cross the line and see Maddie before she's ready. I waited for the text telling me that she can buy her own groceries, but it never came. What I did get was a text thanking me for thinking of them. Progress.

Speaking of my cupcake—

"Hey baby, is everything okay?" I answer my phone.

"Hi handsome, everything's good. I was just wondering something."

"What is it?"

"Would you like to come over and meet Maddie? My brother and sister are here, and I want you to meet them too."

"I'd love to. You want me to come over now?"

"Are you busy? We can wait."

"I'm never too busy for you. I'll be there in thirty minutes."

"Thank you. Please be safe."

"Always. Should I bring my cage so you and Maddie can ride back with me for the barbecue?"

"Sure, I'd like that."

"See you soon, cupcake."

"Bye."

Holy crap. She's finally okay with me meeting Maddie, Carter and Diana. She talks about them all the time. The only ones she doesn't talk about are her parents. I know they're alive, I just don't know where they are. One step at a time.

I hurry and grab my shit, I don't want to keep them waiting. I have a cage—an SUV to drive on rainy days. I don't really enjoy driving it, but for my girls? I'll do anything. Friday morning traffic can suck here in Chicago. Even after regular morning rush hour should be over, it's still horrible. It takes me a little less than thirty minutes to get to Lila's place. And all of a sudden, I'm nervous.

I get out of my cage and walk over to the buzzer box. I press the button for her apartment and wait.

"Hello?" a male voice answers.

"Hey, it's Hollis, here to see Lila."

"Come on up," he says as the buzzer goes off.

I've never been a nervous guy, but this? This makes me nervous. Lila is the youngest, the baby. What if her brother and sister don't like me? Would that make her walk away from me? I guess I'm not so much worried that they'll like me, I'm worried about their thoughts on the club. Lila seems okay with club life, but it's not something that everyone likes or understands. And as much as I know that I need Lila in my life, I could never give up my club.

I get in the elevator and head up to her apartment. Taking a deep breath at her door, I knock. Lila opens the door, and I hesitate. This is new territory for me. I don't know what lines I can or cannot cross yet. So I play it safe and lean in, kissing her on the cheek.

"Mommy? Who's that?" I hear the tiniest voice ask.

That's when I see the most adorable little girl pop her head out from behind Lila. She was hiding behind her, clinging to her leg. I crouch down to her level. She has Lila's caramel-brown eyes and dark hair.

"Hi, I'm Hollis. You must be Maddie." I stick my hand out for her to shake. She looks up at Lila like she's asking permission.

"Hollis is mommy's friend," Lila explains to her. Maddie gives me a smile and gently puts her hand in mine.

"It's very nice to meet you, Maddie." I smile. She giggles at me.

"And this is my brother Carter, and my sister Diana," Lila says.

I stand up and shake both their hands.

"Cimaruta MC?" Carter says.

I nod at him. "Best group around."

He gives me a weird look but doesn't say anything. Great. It looks like he's already made up his mind about me and the club.

Lila

I know the look my brother is giving Hollis. I frown at Carter. I don't care what he thinks he knows about the club, because I can guarantee whatever he's thinking is incorrect. I'm not naïve enough to think the club does nothing wrong. But I do know Charmy, and she would never be with Amante if he wasn't a good person. And at the end of the day, that's what matters most.

My instincts say Hollis is a good man. In the last couple of weeks he's been nothing but a gentleman. And as much as I want to jump into bed with him again, we haven't done anything. He says we already know that part is awesome. And he wants me to be sure before we take it to that level again.

If I'm being honest with myself? I already know what I want. But I'm worried about Maddie. So tonight will tell me what I need to know about Hollis. Being a dad to someone else's baby isn't easy. Especially when the other parent isn't around. It's like you have to compensate for them not being there. There's also the fact that being around a kid once in a while is a totally different thing than being there daily.

Hollis keeps saying I have nothing to worry about. But I need to be sure—for Maddie.

I watch Diana and Hollis talk. Maddie is standing next to Hollis. It's like she's drawn to him, like I am. My brother pulls me to the side.

"Are you sure you want Maddie around a guy like him?" he whispers.

"What do you mean a 'guy like him'?" I raise my eyebrows at Carter.

"He's a biker. With the biggest club in Chicago. They're criminals, Li. What if someone comes after you or Maddie because of him?"

"I appreciate you worrying about us. But Hollis would never let anything like that happen. And what makes you think they're criminals?"

"Come on, Li. We've all grown up hearing the stories about the Cimaruta MC. They're fucking crooks and I don't like it. I don't want you or Maddie around this hooligan."

Oh for fuck's sake, 'hooligan'? Carter has always been protective. But I've never known him to judge someone before getting to know them.

"People can change, Carter. You haven't even

tried to get to know Hollis. Can you at least give him a chance? I really like him."

He sighs and frowns at me. I'm not sure I can convince him, and that makes me angry. I pull Carter into my bedroom.

"You need to stop being a dick. Hollis is a good man. In fact, every member of the Cimaruta MC has been nothing but nice and supportive of Charmaine, and me too. So be the big brother I love and give him a chance. Please."

"And what if he hurts you? Then what? I don't think I can watch you go through that again." He stares at me.

"Pain is part of life, right? We learned that from mom and dad. And I definitely learned that from Travis. So if he hurts me? I'll be okay."

"And if he hurts Maddie?"

"Then I'll kill him."

Carter sighs again. "Okay, sis. For you, I'll give him a chance. One. But if he fucks it up? He won't get another."

I hug him tight. "I'm glad I have you as my brother."

We walk back out and join the others.

"Is everything okay?" Hollis asks as we sit down.

"Everything's good." I smile as we watch Maddie play. "What time do we need to leave?"

"We should get going in a few."

We hang out with Carter and Diana for about an hour before Hollis says we should head out.

"I can watch Maddie if you want," Carter says to me.

"Thank you, big brother. But I want her to meet the rest of the club."

Chapter Eight

Hollis

Having Lila and Maddie at our monthly barbecue is making me want to strut around like a proud peacock with my tail feathers on full display. I have a gorgeous woman and a beautiful daughter. It feels like Maddie's already mine, like Lila is. Watching her run around with my club brothers makes me laugh. My huge biker brothers are falling all over each other, acting like fools just to make a little girl laugh. It's hilarious.

"I can't believe they're doing that for Maddie," Lila says, wrapping her arms around me.

"You're family, cupcake. My family. From this day forward, this club will do anything for you and Maddie. Even if you choose not to be with me."

Holding her close, I can hear her sniffle. I wish she would tell me about her parents. Maybe soon. If anyone knows about having shitty parents, it's me. But then again, maybe she had really good parents and she lost them. Hearing Maddie squeal pulls me out of my thoughts.

"Save me, Hollis!" She giggles as she jumps into my arms. I take off, running away from my brothers, holding Maddie close. She's laughing so hard I'm afraid she's going to pass out. I hide behind Lila as five of my brothers come barreling towards us.

It's like watching a cartoon with the way they try to stop before they knock her over. They end up in a heap, millimeters from Lila's feet. Maddie can't stop laughing, Lila's joined in, and I'm pretty sure I heard her snort which makes everyone within hearing distance start laughing too.

I hug Lila. "You're adorable." I laugh.

"Oh my god, that was embarrassing."

"No way. That was the cutest snort I've ever heard."

She turns to look at me and rolls her eyes. "Snorting is never cute."

"Well I would say I agree, but not after hearing yours." I kiss her before she can respond.

"Unfair." She giggles, then looks up at me. "Being here at the barbecue is different this time. When the MC first invited our group of girls, I thought it would be fun. But it got harder and harder to be here. I watched you all the time. You didn't do anything with the other women, but just seeing them try was rough. I never thought we'd find our way to each other."

"I wish I had known how you felt. If I had, I never would've waited this long to tell you how I feel. I've wanted to be with you since that first night. I just didn't know how to tell you."

"I was worried you thought I was a slut because I went home with you that night."

"I would never think that about you, cupcake." I kiss her and hold her tight.

"I still don't get why you chose me. The women around you are so much more than me."

I frown at her. "What do you mean 'more than you'? You're perfect. Every part of you makes me come alive."

Lila

I'm not usually an insecure person. I know who I am, and I'm okay with me, curves and all. But I'm not everyone's cup of tea, and most guys only really notice me when they're drunk. Hollis makes me feel like I'm the most beautiful woman in the world. When I saw the bunnies around him during those barbecues before, it made me sad. I didn't think he noticed me, and my insecurities crept in. But I realized that I'm the one that pushed him away. If I think back, he did show me that he wanted me from the start. Now I wish I hadn't listened to my fears.

Watching the MC with Maddie makes me feel so loved. None of them have to play with her. But yet here they are, huge biker men playing with a tiny five-year old. As I'm watching them, I see one of Hollis' club brothers walk in. There's a beautiful woman and a little girl with him.

"Come on, cupcake. I want you to meet Bestia and his family. He recently found out that he had a daughter and she and her mama just moved here to Chicago."

"Why didn't he know?"

"It's a long story. Maybe one day Maeve will tell you."

I get it, it's not his place to tell me someone else's story. So I don't push the issue.

"I look forward to getting to know her," I smile and hug him.

"Hey, Bestia," Hollis says as they hug. "This is my Lila and Maddie."

"It's nice to meet you both. This is Maeve and Saoirse." He smiles at us.

"It's very nice to meet you. Your daughter is adorable," Maeve says.

"I love your accent," I say as she chuckles.

"Hi. I'm Saoirse," her daughter says to Maddie.

"Hi. I'm Maddie." She giggles.

"Why don't you two go and play in the bouncy castle?" Bestia suggests.

"Okay, Da," Saoirse says as she grabs Maddie's hand. They run to the castle together.

"I was worried that Saoirse wouldn't have anyone to play with. I'm so glad you and Maddie are here," Maeve says to me.

"I felt the same. Before you got here, the guys were chasing Maddie around. I think they're too big to get into the bouncy castle."

Maeve laughs. "I think they'd pop it if they did."

"Hey! I can get into the castle without popping it," Bestia says. He kisses her, then heads over to the castle.

We all follow him. This is going to be epic. We watch him get into the castle with the girls. After a few minutes, there's a popping noise followed by the sound of air escaping, and the castle starts to tip over.

"You broke the castle, Da!" Saoirse is giggling as she and Maddie crawl out of the entrance.

"Wow. You broke the kids' bouncy castle," Giustizia teases his twin.

"Shut up." Bestia laughs. "We'll fix it."

We sit and watch the guys start looking for the hole. It takes a little while, but they finally find it and attempt to make a seal. It takes a few tries but they get it fixed, and the girls go back in to play.

Chapter Nine

Lila

Today is the first day that Hollis is coming with me to take Maddie to school. In these last few weeks, she's gotten super attached to him. When I watch them together, it makes my heart happy. Hollis never gets tired of her or acts like she's being annoying with her endless questions. I hate that she's missed out on all this stuff because Travis decided to fuck someone else. After he left, I spent months trying to find him. But either no one really knew anything or they didn't want to tell me. Which in hindsight was probably a good thing, because that's when I found out he'd been cheating on me.

"Are you okay, cupcake?" he asks, snapping me out of my pity party.

"Yeah, it's just sometimes I still wonder why Travis left us the way he did. How could he leave Maddie? The one thing I'm grateful for is that she doesn't remember him. And the few times she asked where her daddy was, I just told her that he had to go away and maybe one day he'd be back. I never wanted to lie to her. Even if it hurt me."

Hollis wraps his arms around me. "You're the best mom Maddie could ever have. No matter what life has thrown at you, you've always done what's best for her. Maddie is a lucky little girl."

"Now that we have you, we're both lucky. We should get going, morning traffic is crap around the school."

"Okay, baby," he says as he stretches. Then he gets up and heads into the bathroom. "I'll be out in a few minutes."

I watch him walk away. I love watching his butt flex when he walks. I think his muscles have muscles. A lot of the MC guys are built like my Hollis, like it's a prerequisite to be a part of the club or something. Muscular, tattoos, and sexy as sin.

I stretch and roll out of bed to follow him into the bathroom. We've gotten pretty comfortable around each other. Well, enough to brush our teeth and shower together. We still haven't had sex again, even with all the showers and teasing. I love that Hollis is letting me take this slow. I told him I'd like us to get to know each other better first.

I watch him shower through the glass doors. Times like this make me want to rethink the no sex rule. Damn him with his sexy muscles and tight ass. Okay. Look away, Lila. I finish brushing my teeth and go to wake Maddie up.

"Come on Maddie, time to get up," I say as I kiss her tiny face.

"So early, Mama." She yawns.

"Same time every school day, munchkin."

She giggles and rolls out of bed.

"Make sure you brush your teeth and then come down for breakfast," I say to her as I leave her room.

"Okay Mama, I set my quacky timer."

Hollis bought her a timer that has a baby duck pop up every thirty seconds, making a quacking sound. It helps Maddie brush her teeth.

Thirty seconds in each section of her mouth. It's also made her start quacking at everything. And when I say everything, I mean everything.

"We should get a puppy," Hollis says as he comes into the kitchen.

"Whoa. A puppy? Um. Why?"

"Because all kids should have a pet, and a puppy seems like a good fit for Maddie."

"I don't think I can handle a puppy."

"You wouldn't have to do it alone. I'm here to help you. I also wanted to ask you something."

He seems nervous now. I've never seen him get nervous about anything. I stare at him, trying to figure out what he could be so nervous about. Is he leaving me?

"What's wrong? Did something happen?" I ask.

Hollis

"No, cupcake. Nothing's wrong. I just wanted to ask you to move in with me. You and Maddie," I blurt out as fast as I can. She opens her mouth to say something. "Before you say no, please give me a second to say what I need to. Look, I know it's fast. When Luciana met Rónán, they fell in love so fast I thought they were crazy. Then Amante and Charmaine. Again, crazy. But they met the same night we did. And I fought that feeling as much as I could because it scared the shit out of me. But now I realize I can't fight it—I don't want to fight it. You're it for me, Lila. You, Maddie and all the other babies we'll have. So move in with me so we can start our life together."

Now that I word-vomited all over her, I watch as she processes all of it. I'm not sure if her silence is a good or bad thing. And now it's making me anxious. Dammit. Did I just fuck this up?

"You want more babies?" she whispers.

"Hell yes, cupcake. I want as many babies as you'll say yes to."

Lila gives me a huge smile. "Why don't we talk to Maddie and see what she thinks."

I nod at her. "I know she'll say yes."

"So confident," she teases.

I nibble her ear and that makes her giggle. It's one of my favorite sounds.

"I'm hungry!" we hear Maddie say as she runs into the kitchen.

"Can I ask her?" I ask Lila. She nods and smiles.

"Hey, Maddie."

"Hey, Hollis," she mimics me as she giggles.

I tickle her and scoop her up, setting her on one of the chairs.

"I have a question for you. What would you say if I asked you and your mommy to come live with me?"

"You mean at your house?" she asks.

"Yes. At my house."

"Like a sleepover?"

"No. Well kind of. You wouldn't come back here. You and Mommy would stay with me forever."

Maddie looks a little puzzled. "But we live here."

"You do right now. But I want you to come live with me, if that's okay."

"Okay. Can we have pancakes now?"

I chuckle. "Yes, I think your mommy's done cooking them."

The three of us sit down and eat breakfast together. We talk about how Maddie wants to decorate her room and what new movies we should get. I think I'm going to like family life.

"You gotta get dressed for school. Do you

need help picking something out?" Lila asks Maddie.

"No, I got it, Mommy." She smiles as she hops down from her chair.

"Dishes first, please."

I can't stop smiling as I look at my two girls. I'm damn lucky. We watch Maddie put her dishes in the dishwasher then hop away to her room.

"I think she was kind of sticky from the syrup." I chuckle.

"Wash your face and hands first!" Lila calls out. I laugh as we hear a little sigh, then the water running in the bathroom.

"So when should we start moving you in? Today?"

Lila laughs. "You want to start today? I haven't even talked to my landlord yet."

"Okay well...we can talk to your landlord after we take Maddie to school and then my brothers will come help us move. We can be done today."

Her eyes get really wide. "Are you serious? I mean, are you really sure you're ready for this? Like right now?"

"Cupcake, I've been sure since the night we

met. I may have fought it a little at the start, but I knew you were the one."

"But being with us twenty-four seven is different from what we've been doing. I need you to be absolutely sure, because of Maddie."

"Baby, Maddie is mine too. That little girl will never feel unloved or unwanted by me or my club."

I know that Lila is worried not just for Maddie, but for herself. After her ex left, she found out he'd been cheating. The other night she finally told me his full name and I have Salvatore Mancini looking into it. I want to know everything about the asshole who hurt my girls. So far, Sal has gotten enough information that if he ever bothers us, I know where to find him. He has a family—a wife and three kids. The oldest kid—a boy, is about a year younger than Maddie. Which means he was born while Travis was still with Lila. We're trying to find out if the boy is his or not. If he is Travis' kid, I have to tell Lila. That's not going to be an easy conversation.

From what she's told me, Travis has never paid a dime in child support. When they divorced, Travis never asked for custody or visitation. So he hasn't seen Maddie since the day he left. I think that hurt Lila just as much as finding out he was cheating. She does have a court order for child support. He's supposed to pay three hundred dollars every month. According to the court documents, when he left them, he was a mechanic and was making good money. So as of now, he owes them thousands. Lila hasn't wanted to push it—I think she's afraid that he'll retaliate by trying to take Maddie. That'll never happen. I *will* kill him if he touches either of them.

Chapter Ten

Lila

After dropping Maddie off at school and signing the papers to allow Hollis to be able to drop her off and pick her up, we go back to my place. My landlord lives in the building next door to our triplex, so we're going to go talk to him in person. My lease has been month-to-month for a while now. But my landlord is good people. It's him, his wife and their two kids. They've never raised our rent during the whole two years that we've been living here. Part of me is sad to leave this place. When my siblings and I moved out of the house we grew up in, we found this triplex. We've never lived apart from each other. But knowing that Hollis wants us makes me feel like I'm on top of the world.

Hollis comes around and opens my door. He takes my hand—I love the little things he does for me. We head to my landlord's apartment and knock on his door.

"Lila!" Martin says as he gives me a hug.

"Hi, Martin. This is my boyfriend, Hollis," I say as I hug him back.

"Nice to meet you, Hollis," he says. As they shake hands, he takes a second to look at the patches on the front of Hollis' cut. "Cimaruta, huh?"

"Yes sir. Nice to meet you too," Hollis says.

"Martin! Where are your manners? Come in," Maria, Martin's wife, says as she pushes him out of the way.

We laugh and follow them inside.

"Is everything okay, Lila?" Maria asks me.

"Everything's great. I wanted to come and talk to you because Hollis asked me to move in with him. So I'll be moving out as soon as possible."

Martin is still staring at Hollis. I'm guessing it's because of his cut? I wish he would stop.

"This is really sudden, are you sure?" Martin asks, and Maria slaps his arm.

"I appreciate everything you both have done for me, and for Maddie. But I'm sure." I smile at them as Hollis takes my hand.

"I'll take good care of my girls," Hollis says.

I can see the hard look on Maria's face softening. It's like she's seeing Hollis as I see him. The handsome, protective man who would do anything for Maddie and me.

"You *better* take good care of them. They're good girls and deserve only the best," Maria says to Hollis.

"I couldn't agree more. We should get going, we have a lot to do today."

I nod at Hollis and give Maria and Martin another hug. Hollis shakes Martin's hand and Maria pulls him in for a hug.

"You bring Maddie over so we can say a proper goodbye. And I know the kids will want to see you too." Maria smiles.

"I'll bring her by before we're done moving."

We head up to my apartment and I see the guys from the MC waiting. I look at Hollis and he smiles at me.

"I told you they'd be here to help."

I laugh at all of them. "Thank you so much for helping us."

They each give me a hug and say that this is what families do. It makes me feel all warm and fuzzy.

Everyone gets to work packing up my apartment. I don't have much—we've never had the money to buy a lot of things. I've always made sure Maddie had everything she needed, but the extras were saved for birthdays and Christmas.

Hollis

My brothers have gotten almost everything moved out of Lila's place. She doesn't really have much and I plan to remedy that. My girls are going to have everything they want, not just things they need. I'll make sure of that.

"Cupcake, it's time to get our girl. Do you want to keep working and I'll go get her?" I ask Lila.

"That would be great, if you don't mind."

"Of course not. I'll be right back. Do you want lunch? I can pick something up."

"That sounds good. I wasn't hungry until you said that." She laughs.

I let my brothers know I'll be grabbing lunch for everyone and get in my cage to pick Maddie up. The drive to Maddie's school used to take about thirty minutes. But now that they live with me, it's only fifteen minutes. I pull into the parking lot to wait. I've got ten minutes before school is out. Lila said she goes in about five minutes prior.

> Hollis: Just got here. I'll start walking in a couple minutes

> Lila: Okay. Thank you for picking her up. And thank you for everything

> Hollis: I told you, cupcake. You and Maddie are my girls. You don't have to worry about anything anymore

> Lila: (heart emoji)

I head inside, stopping at the office to sign in. Everyone who comes into the school has to go through the office first. Then I walk to Maddie's classroom. When I get there, I look inside. I don't see her right away and I get a weird feeling in my stomach. Maybe she's just not visible from where I'm standing. Other parents are starting to gather outside the classrooms. Some stare at me, but I've gotten used to it. Some are curious and some look judgy. Fuck the judgers.

The kids start coming out of Maddie's classroom, but there's no Maddie. What the fuck is going on? I walk in to ask her teacher.

"Hi, I'm Hollis and I'm here for Madeleine Slater."

The teacher stares at me with a shocked look on her face. Which is comical because I just saw her this morning when we dropped Maddie off.

"S-she was picked up earlier. H-he said he was her father and that it was an emergency. Something had happened to her mother," she stutters.

Holy fuck. What is going on? Is this school so incompetent that they don't follow their own fucking rules? I'm going to suggest moving Maddie to a different school immediately.

"Only two people are allowed to pick Maddie up. Me, and her mother. Not even her aunt or uncle are on that list!" At this point I'm yelling and I don't give a fuck. The teacher starts crying, but I don't care. She can cry all she wants —she's the one who fucked up.

"Sir, you can't come in here and start yelling at our teachers."

Oh good. The principal is here to stick his nose in.

"I wouldn't have to yell if you ran your school the right fucking way."

"You don't need to use that kind of language."

"Fuck you. You and your staff let someone take my child. There are two names on the list for pickup, and that's me and her mother. I know where her mother is because I was just with her, and I'm standing in front of you. So where is my daughter?" I get right in his face and I can see the fear in his eyes. He waits until the other parents and kids are out of the area before addressing the situation.

The principal turns to the teacher and asks her what happened. She explains to him that she got a message to bring Maddie to the office because her dad was there to pick her up early. And so she did.

"Did you see the guy who was waiting?" I ask her and she nods. "I'm calling the police."

"Wait, we can handle this. There's no need to call the police."

"No. You've done enough," I snap as I get my phone out to call Salvatore.

"Hello?" he answers.

"Hey Sal, it's Cavallo. I need you to come down to Walden Elementary. My daughter was taken. Please hurry."

"Your daughter? Wait, nevermind. We're on our way."

"Thank you."

And then I realize I have to call Lila. Fuck. I call Fantasma first.

"What's up, Cavallo? You get lost on your way back?" he jokes.

"Maddie is missing," I say, trying to keep my voice steady.

"What the fuck are you talking about?"

"When I got here her teacher said her dad picked her up already. They just fucking let it happen. I called Sal and he's on his way. I need you to bring Lila

here. I don't want to leave in case they find something. But I can't tell her over the phone."

"I got you, brother. We'll be there soon. Just breathe. We'll find her."

"I'm more worried about how Lila is going to take this."

"I know. We'll all be here for her. See you soon."

I hang up and wait for Sal to arrive. He and his partner, Mac, pull up and park in record time.

"What happened?" Sal asks.

I tell him the story that the teacher told me just as Fantasma pulls into the parking lot with Lila. She jumps out before he can get the car fully parked and runs over to me.

"Where's Maddie? What happened?" She's getting hysterical.

"Take a deep breath, cupcake." I breathe with her.

"I-is she dead?" She starts to cry.

I look at her. I don't want to lie, because I don't know what's happened yet.

"I don't think so. Someone picked her up already. They said it was her dad."

"Do you have a picture of her uh, bio dad?" Salvatore asks.

"I-I'm sure I have one at the apartment."

"If you want, I'll have the guys look for it. Is it in a box?" I ask her.

She nods. "It's in a box labeled 'Travis'. I kept a few things for Maddie in case she ever asked about him when she got older," she says softly.

I hold her tight as we listen to Fantasma tell the guys at the apartment what to look for.

"Do you really think it was him?" she asks me.

"I don't know, baby. But we need to make sure either way."

She starts sobbing and I hold her tighter.

"We're going to find her. I promise you that."

What I do know is whoever took my Maddie is going to pay for it. That much I can promise Lila. I'm not saying it out loud. But it's still a promise.

Chapter Eleven

Lila

It's been eight hours since Travis took my baby. The police have been looking for them, but so far no one knows where they are. Thankfully, there was video from the school proving it was Travis and his wife. Salvatore has been keeping us updated, and so far we think he's still in the city. They're monitoring the train stations and the airport. They had him on traffic cams, but lost him about six blocks from the school. There's also been an amber alert sent out for my baby. But so far she hasn't been spotted. I know the statistics. I may never see my daughter again and it's killing me.

Hollis has been by my side constantly, I know he wants to be with his club and the police looking for our baby. But I need him here with me. Besides Hollis, my girls have been with me as much as they can, but the only thing I can do is cry. I want my daughter home. I don't know why Travis would take her, he never indicated he wanted her after he left us.

"You need to eat something. I know it's not what you want to do, but you need to keep your strength up," Luciana says to me.

I've gotten to know Luciana and her twin Isabella. They've been here keeping me company and trying to stop me from worrying too much. They're part of Hollis' MC family and I'm so grateful for them. They've sat here with me even though all I can do is curl up into a ball and cry. I sip at the soup that Luciana brought me.

"Thank you. You really don't have to stay with me, I'm okay."

"Nope. You're stuck with us. I told Cavallo someone would always be here with you," she says. "I don't know how you feel right now. But I know how much you love Maddie, how much we all love her. We will find her."

I've learned a few things about the Cimaruta MC. When they say you're family, they mean it. Every one of them is willing to bend over backwards to help no matter what it is you need. They also like to hover and hug. Which isn't bad, I'm just not used to it. My parents didn't hug us much. I hug Maddie all the time because I want her to know how much I love her. Maddie. Why would Travis take her? And why now?

There's so many fucking questions that I don't have answers for and it's making me crazy. Travis has his own family. He has zero need for my Maddie. Salvatore showed me the file they have on him. He has a wife. I'm guessing she's who he left me for, and three children. And if the oldest is biologically his? That means he was cheating on me longer than I thought, which in hindsight doesn't really matter anymore. But it still pisses me off.

A knock at the door pulls me out of my misery.

"I'll get it," Luciana says. "You need to eat."

I sigh and keep eating the soup. It does taste really good and I know if I don't finish it, she'll just come back and make me. So I continue eating as I hear Sal's voice getting closer.

"Did you find her?" I blurt out.

He gives me a sad look. "Not yet. But we did find something interesting. It looks like they had a baby recently, a little girl. She passed away a few weeks after she was born. The death certificate cites SIDS as the cause of death."

"That's sad. But what does that have to do with my Maddie?"

"It was a girl. The only girl they had. The other three are boys. I'm wondering if the reason he took Maddie was because they wanted a girl."

"What the fuck? You really think he would do that?" Luciana frowns.

"Grief does things to people. I've heard stories like this before," Sal explains. "You'd be shocked to know what desperate people will do. And if that's the case here, it might be a good thing. That might mean she's being taken care of and not hurt."

I don't know what to say to that so I just stay quiet.

"That is fucking nuts," Isabella says. "We need to find them. Are you sure they're still in Chicago?"

"I won't lie, I'm not one hundred percent sure of anything. But I can say for certain that we won't stop looking for her," he says.

"It's been eight hours. I've read the statistics,"

I say as my voice catches. "After twenty-four hours, the chances of finding her decreases significantly."

Hollis wraps his arms around me. "You can't think like that, baby. We're going to find her and bring her home."

Hollis

I hate that we don't know where Travis has taken Maddie. He must have planned this in advance, because they moved out of their rental. I hate having to leave my girl, but we have church tonight and I can't not go.

"I'll be back soon. Sal is going to stay with you," I say to Lila. She nods at me as I lean in to kiss her.

"Thank you," she says softly. "I don't think I could do this without you."

"You never have to thank me for being here for you. I will always be here."

I head over to the clubhouse with Fuoco and Dolce. It's not far from my house, two minutes on the four-wheeler. After we all pack ourselves into the room where we hold church, we find our seats and sit down at the table.

Forza bangs his gavel.

"I called this emergency meeting to discuss what's going on with Cavallo and his family. It's been almost nine hours since Maddie's bio donor took her. I've called the Mancini family. They're headed here now with the Southside Mafia. I figured we need as much help as we can get."

"Thank you, Forza. I just wish we knew more," I say. Everyone nods in agreement.

There's a knock at the door, and Fantasma gets up to open it. The Mancinis and the Southside Mafia come into the room. The Mancinis are a mafia family and have been for a long time. Their founders came from Italy and Ireland, like the founders of our club. Enea Mancini is now the head of their family.

His wife Gráinne, and our Forte grew up together back in Ireland, and then reconnected here in Chicago about four years ago. Whenever either family needs help, the other is there. No questions asked, and no matter what needs to be done.

And now they're here for me and my family.

"Enea, thank you for coming." Forza shakes his hand, then shakes the hand of the head of the

Southside Mafia, Elio Salvadori. "Elio, thank you as well. And thanks to all of you for coming to help us look for little Maddie."

We met the Southside Mafia earlier this year, when Fuoco was kidnapped. This time, Elio has brought his consigliere and two of his capos.

Forza goes over what we know about Maddie's kidnapping, and all the information we have on Travis and his wife.

"Wait. Is it really possible this asshole stole Maddie because he lost his other kid? What the fuck is wrong with him? And his wife just went along with it?" Mitchell 'Granchio' Harris, one of our enforcers, frowns. "What kind of people are they? She's a baby. And she's not his."

I love my club brothers and sisters. The anger I feel toward Travis and his wife is mirrored on the faces of my family. We need to find my Maddie.

"Do we have a plan?" Carlo Fenati, Elio's consigliere, asks.

"Not yet," Forza answers.

"Does the little one have a tracker?" Elio asks.

The tracker that Elio is asking about is something we all have. It's an implant that's hidden just under the skin in case of something like this.

"No. Lila and Maddie are new to our family," Forza says. "We haven't been able to discuss the trackers yet, and why they're so important."

Elio nods. "Okay, so what do we know about possible locations? Does Lila know of any place they might go? Maybe a house the shitbag's family owns? Or the psycho wife's family?"

"She told Salvatore that his family doesn't own property here. But she doesn't know anything about the wife. Sal is looking into her now."

"If it's okay, I would like Mario to trace their path from the school to where they were lost on the cameras," Elio says.

Forza nods and gives Mario the video footage we have. "Maybe fresh eyes will help. It's been almost ten hours now."

I get a text from Sal asking if he can come into the room and I let Forza know.

"Let him in," Forza says to Fantasma.

Sal comes in and shakes everyone's hands. "I have an update on Travis and his family. They were seen going through the toll from Naperville back to Chicago."

"Can I see the footage? Were you able to see the license or at least the make of the car? Color?" Mario asks.

"We got the plate and ran it already. Here's the address the car is registered to, but we already checked it out. From what we know, they moved out last week. But I have an officer sitting on the house. No one's been back since we've been watching it."

"Fuck. So now what?" I frown.

"Now you give me the footage and I will get one of my guys to see if we can find the car," Mario says.

Sal nods and hands him a flash drive. "I know It's pointless to say come to me before going after them. But can you at least give me a heads up?"

"We'll let you know what we find," Forza says.

"Thank you." Sal nods. "And if you need anything, let me know. I need to go back to the station."

"Thanks, Sal," I say as I stand to shake his hand.

He hugs me instead. "We're going to find her."

I nod and take a deep breath. "I just hope he doesn't hurt her."

"My gut is still telling me that he wants her to replace the baby they lost."

"Yeah, that's what mine is saying too. It's just

so fucking hard to sit here and wait. I need to be out there looking for my daughter. And what if Maddie fights back?"

Sal doesn't even blink an eye when I call Maddie my daughter.

"She's going to be okay. I'll be in touch if I find anything else," he says as he leaves with his partner.

"Okay, I think we're all up to date. I want everyone who is able out there looking for them. We don't know if Travis knows that Lila is with you or not. I would assume that if he did, he wouldn't have touched Maddie. But I can't say that for sure. Either way, we won't stop till we find her."

Everyone pounds their fists on the table, agreeing with Forza.

"I want to thank all of you for helping Lila and me find Maddie."

"Family," Fuoco says. Everyone stands and agrees. Family. I don't know what I'd do without them.

Chapter Twelve

Travis

When my wife, Shawna, and I decided to get Madeleine, I didn't know my ex was involved with that fucking criminal. Now that I do know, I'm convinced we did the right thing. My daughter will not be raised around that 'club'. I know about their reputation. The kicker is that I want to be with Lila. I've never loved Shawna, I only stayed because of the kids. Every time I thought of leaving, she got pregnant again. She threatened to take them away from me if I left her. The only woman I've ever loved was Lila

Slater. She even kept my last name when we got divorced. That has to mean something, right?

The school that Lila picked was so easy to get into. I made up a story about Madeleine's mom being in the emergency room. They brought her to me and we left. They didn't even ask Maddie if she knew me or not.

When Maddie realized something was wrong, I told her that her mom didn't want her anymore and asked me to take care of her. Of course it was all a lie, but she's a kid. How much can she really understand? And Shawna convinced me we deserve her. We lost our little girl almost a month ago and it's been the worst time of our lives. But now we have another little girl and our family is complete.

"Are you hungry? I can make you a sandwich," I hear Shawna say to Maddie.

"I want my mommy. Why won't you take me to my mommy?" She sobs.

"Your daddy already told you. Your mommy doesn't want you anymore. She told your daddy and me that she wants you to live with us now."

"You said my mommy doesn't love me, but you're lying! My mommy loves me more than anything. She tells me every day!" Maddie yells at Shawna.

"I'm your mommy now. And you will not yell at me," she snaps back. I walk in to see her pick Madeleine up and put her in the room we prepared for her, locking it from the outside. Madeleine pounds on the door and screams how much she hates us.

"You need to either shut her up or soundproof that room. Otherwise, someone is going to call the cops," she yells at me.

"Why are you yelling at me?" I frown.

"She's your daughter. You need to control her."

"She's your daughter too. If you remember, this is what you wanted. So figure it out."

I watch my wife open the bedroom door and slap Maddie across the face.

"Stop your screaming right fucking now. Or I will tape your mouth shut and tie you to the fucking bed." She walks out and slams the door, then locks it again.

"I didn't mean for you to fucking hit her. She's just a kid," I yell at Shawna. I've never seen her hit our boys like that. Even when they were throwing their own tantrums.

"Well she stopped, right? Your bitch ex probably let her get away with everything. That's why she's a fucking brat. She'll learn to obey us."

I sigh and sit on the couch. I need to figure out how to get us out of Illinois. When we came up with our plan to bring Maddie home with us, I had to make sure they couldn't trace us. We got out of our apartment lease and are staying in a weekly rental. They don't ask questions. Our boys are on a trip to Montana with some friends of ours. They won't be back for another week, which is perfect. By then, we'll be out of Chicago. When they come home, the plan is to tell them that Lila didn't want Maddie anymore and that she's going to be living with us from now on.

I have no doubt Lila and her criminal boyfriend are looking for Maddie. As I'm trying to think things through, I see Shawna take something out of the closet. It looks like a gun case. But why would she have a gun?

I've loved Lila since we were kids, and one day that love felt different, so I kissed her. It was the best decision of my life. Then at seventeen, Lila got pregnant. It scared the shit out of me, but I was happy. We had Madeleine right after we graduated high school. Then one stupid mistake brought Shawna and I together. I went out with my friends and drank too much—fake IDs were the thing back then. We were celebrating graduating high school and ended up at a strip club. It was a simple lap dance that started it. My friends thought it would be fun for each of us to get one. So of course like an asshole, I let it happen, even though I knew Lila would be pissed. Shawna danced for all of us, then did a lap dance for each of us privately. We ended up fucking during my lap dance. The condom I had in my wallet was old because it's not something I had to worry about with Lila. And to be honest, I forgot I even had it in there. So of course it failed, and Shawna got pregnant.

I didn't find out until after my son was born. I ran into Shawna at the store one day. I didn't recognize her, but she recognized me. My boy wasn't with her at the time, but she made it a point to tell me and gave me her number. I was fucking scared. On one hand, if she was telling the truth, I had to decide what to do and how to tell Lila. On the other hand, if she was lying, I still had to tell Lila. There was no way I could just sit and wonder if that kid was mine. I was fucked either way.

The kid turned out to be mine and I was more fucked than I originally thought. I knew the minute Lila found out, she'd leave me and take my daughter with her. Could I blame her? No. I was the one who fucked up. So I did the only rational thing I could think of. I left her first. And in doing so, I destroyed the only real thing that ever mattered to me. And now Lila is with that biker asshole and I've kidnapped my own daughter to make my current wife happy. I'm fucked again.

Hollis

Today reminds me of the day Luciana was kidnapped. It's been six months since that happened. I now know what Forza and Forte went through while waiting to find her. It's the worst. I want to be out there searching, but I'm here with Lila because that's what she asked me to do.

"Baby? I know you want me here with you. But I need to be out there searching for our Maddie. I can't just sit here and let the rest of them do all the work. Luciana, Isabella and Caitríona will be here with you. But I have to go.

I love you and Maddie too much to not do everything I can to find her."

Lila looks at me and nods. "I know you need to be out there. Go. Find our baby. Please." She starts sobbing and I want to kill Travis for doing this to my woman. In fact, I think I will when we find him.

I kiss Lila and hug her tight. Then I hand her over to Caitríona who holds her while she cries. It breaks my heart to leave her, but I need this. I rush back to the clubhouse to talk with my brothers.

"Mario is in the tech room going over all the footage. Sebastiano Mancini is in there with Bestia. The Mancini women are headed to your house to keep Lila company," Forza says.

"They're already there. What's our next step? Are we waiting for more intel? There's got to be something we can do."

"Calm down, Cavallo. Take a breath. We need to get more information. If we just go out and ride around, we might get lucky and catch them. But chances are we won't, and then we might be too far away when we get a solid lead."

I know Forza is right. But I just can't sit here and wait. What if Travis is hurting Maddie? What if his wife is? All these fucking what ifs.

"I think we found something," we hear Sebastiano call out to us.

We all run to the tech room to see what they found. Please let it be a lead to my baby.

"We looked at all the different routes he could've taken that have cameras at those intersections. And Sal got us into the traffic cams. That looks like the same car here at the Sandlot apartments."

"It does look like their car. Okay, we need a plan," Forza says.

"Mario, you and Carlo take two of the Cimaruta and head over there. Confirm it's them and make sure they don't leave. The rest of us will get everything together." Elio takes charge.

Mario and Carlo nod.

"Giustizia and Raziel, you two go with them. We'll be there soon. Don't let them see you. We don't know if he knows about the connection to the club," Forza says.

I leave the room and head to our armory vault. Raziel and Giustizia follow me so they can grab our thermal gun. They're also loading up on weapons and body armor.

"Don't worry, brother. We're gonna bring your daughter home safe. Today," Giustizia says as he hugs me.

"Thank you," I choke out. My emotions are all over the place.

When we head back out to the group, everyone is almost ready.

"Should we call Sal?" Bestia asks.

"Yes. Call him and give him a heads up. Cavallo, go to Lila and tell her what we know and come right back. We need to leave ASAP."

I nod at Forza and speed back to my house to tell my girl what's going on.

"Did you find her?" Lila blurts out as I walk in the door.

"We're pretty sure we found Travis' car. Some of the guys are headed there now. I need you to stay here."

"I can't stay here, Hollis. What if it is them? Maddie needs me."

"Of course she does. But I don't know what's going to happen when we get there. And I can't be worrying about her safety and yours at the same time. I need to be able to focus on her, knowing you're safe here. Please, baby."

It takes all of us to convince Lila that it's best for her to stay here. But in the end, she relents. I just hope she really does understand why I want her to stay. I need to focus on Maddie and making sure she's not hurt—no matter what happens.

Heading back to the clubhouse, I keep running through different scenarios in my head. There are only two that I like, and they involve Travis and his wife dead or in jail. Either will do for me, as long as they never come near my Lila or my Maddie again.

"Mario checked in and said it's definitely their car. They don't know if their boys or Maddie are in the apartment yet. They're working on the thermal imaging as we speak. Best case scenario, we'll be able to pinpoint everyone in there," Elio says.

"Okay people, everyone wears armor. No excuses. Remember they have three young boys as well. We're not sure if they're in there, but we have to proceed like they are."

Everyone nods and we head out in some of our cages. Our bikes will make too much noise and we can't take the chance they'll hear them and run.

When we get to the apartment complex, we make sure to cover the obvious entrances and exits. My main concern is the kids. Not only do I not want Maddie hurt, I don't want their other kids to get hurt either.

Salvatore and his partner arrive just as we're about to head up to the apartment.

"Fuck," Mario says.

"Don't worry, we're not here to mess up your plans. We're here for back up and to clear the building. There are six other apartments and we need to make sure they're all vacated. Quietly."

I know that it pulls at Salvatore in situations like this. He's a cop. But he also grew up in the Mancini mafia so he understands. I asked him once why he chose to be a cop. He told me it was because he knew one day his family would need one, and he was going to be the one to help them. He's a good man. He and his partner clear the building as quickly and quietly as they can.

"Raziel, you and Mario take the front door. Bestia, you and Giustizia take the back. The rest of us will be in position."

"The thermal is showing two people in the front room. And from the layout we've seen of the apartments, there are two bedrooms towards the back. There's a heat signature in one of the back rooms," Fantasma says.

"I need to be part of this," I say to Forza as I start walking toward Raziel.

He grabs my shoulder and shakes his head at

me. "You're too close to this. I need you here so I can make sure you don't do anything foolish."

As much as I want to fight him, I don't. Not just because he's my president, but because he's right. I would probably barge in there, guns blazing, and get myself or Maddie hurt. So I nod at Forza and step back.

We watch as Raziel and Mario walk up to the front door. A woman answers, who I'm assuming is Travis' wife, Shawna. We can't hear the conversation they're having, but it looks like she's getting annoyed. And now she's yelling at them and trying to shut the door.

"Shit. She has a gun in her hand," Sal says quietly into our coms as he and his partner start moving towards the building.

I've never been a religious person, but I pray to whoever is listening to please keep my Maddie safe. I don't think Lila will be able to handle it if something happens to her.

"I have to call this in. She definitely has a gun," Sal reports quietly.

What happens next feels like it's in slow motion. I've been in gun fights, bar fights, you name it. But I've never been in one where I was this concerned for someone else.

Shawna lifts the gun, points it at Mario and

screams at him to get off her doorstep. When he doesn't, she fires at him and he falls to the ground. She turns wildly to Raziel and he goes down too. She puts another round into each of them, then whips around to aim at something inside the apartment. But before she can get another shot off, she collapses. The bullet came from Salvatore's partner, Mac.

A man comes running to the door and drops to his knees next to Shawna. I recognize Travis from the picture that Lila showed me. Bestia and Giustizia get on their coms and let us know they're breaching the back door. Salvatore and Mac run to secure Travis, who doesn't resist when they cuff him. We hear sirens getting closer.

Forza finally nods at me and I sprint to the apartment. The moment I'm through the doorway, I hear a tiny voice call my name. My Maddie. I kneel down and she runs into my arms.

"I knew you would come for me," she whispers. She's shaking as I hold her tight. My tears fall on her hair. This little girl is everything to me. And now it's time to take her home to her mama.

Chapter Fourteen

Hollis

These last few weeks have been the hardest I've ever had to deal with. Maddie hasn't gone back to school yet. But Lila did agree to move Maddie to a one. It's the same school as Francesco's daughter, Saoirse. They both start today, and we're all a little nervous. The first week after Maddie was kidnapped, she had nightmares every night. By the second week it slowed down, but I know she's still scared.

Even though Mario and Raziel were wearing kevlar vests, they still took hits from Shawna. Mario took two bullets, one in the upper thigh, and one in the shoulder. Raziel took one in the shoulder too, and the second one grazed his other arm. Thank god that bitch wasn't a good shot or we would've lost them. They were both released from the hospital last week.

Travis is being held without bail. He's charged with kidnapping a minor, holding a minor hostage, and running from the police. They haven't said how much time he'll get for all that. But I'm not worried. Let that fucking asshole try and come near any of us when he gets out. He has a price on his head and I'm pretty sure he knows it. His wife got off easy and died at the scene. She's the one who put hands on my daughter, and if she wasn't dead? Her time in prison would not have been fun.

I kiss Lila's head and wrap my arms around her tighter. She wiggles her ass and my cock hardens so fast my head feels light.

"Baby," I whisper.

I hear her soft giggle as she moves her ass more. Oh, okay. That's the game she wants to play this morning. I've been patient. But I want her so fucking bad. I slide my hand down her stomach. When I reach her pussy, I find she's not wearing any underwear. Fuck me.

I slowly slide my finger into her pussy as she moans.

"I need you, Hollis."

These are the words I've been waiting to hear from my cupcake. I flip her so she's on her back and pull her night shirt off.

"Fuck, you're beautiful."

"Curves and all?" she asks, sounding uncertain.

I look at her. "Everything about you is perfect. Especially your curves."

I kiss and lick my way to her breasts and give each one the attention they deserve. She starts moaning as she pulls at my shirt. I stop long enough to help her get it off. My boxers are next. I smile as she stares at my cock.

"Fuck, I missed you," she says as she reaches for my cock, then licks it slowly from tip to base.

"Baby." I moan. "I need you to stop. I want to be in you when I come."

She gives me one last lick and lets go. I kiss her stomach and make my way to her pussy.

"Fucking gorgeous." I moan as I slide my tongue between her folds. Then I suck on her clit as I slide my finger into her pussy.

"Oh God, baby, I'm gonna come. Fuck!"

I lick up her juices as she comes down from

her orgasm. Then I work my way back up her body and line my cock up with her pussy. I start to push in—I don't want to hurt her, so I go as slow as I can. Holy fuck, I feel like I'm gonna bust my fucking nut and only the tip of my cock is in her.

"Are you okay?" I ask her.

"Yes. Please baby, I need you to fuck me." She gasps.

I keep pushing till I'm all the way in. She feels like fucking heaven.

"Baby, I'm not going to last. You feel too fucking good." I growl as I move faster.

"Come for me, baby." She moans.

I hold her tight as my cum shoots into her. She's milking everything out of me as I try to keep my weight off her. I don't want to break our connection just yet.

"Baby, I didn't even think," I say as I pant.

She gives me a puzzled look.

"I didn't wear a condom. I'm clean, but I wanted to be inside you so bad, I didn't even think about it. I'm sorry."

"It's ok. I'm on the pill and I'm clean." She smiles and kisses me.

Part of me is sad that she's on the pill. Having a baby with Lila is something I want.

And now would be as good a time as any to start.

I smile and finally roll off her. "I love you, Lila."

She props herself up on my chest. "I love you, Hollis. Thank you for loving me and Maddie."

"I will always love you and Maddie. You're both mine forever. Marry me."

Lila

Holy shit, did he just ask me to marry him?

"Yes, cupcake. I'm serious. I want us to be a family. Marry me. Let me adopt Maddie."

When we first hooked up, I didn't know if he took me home because he was drunk, or if he really liked me. These last few weeks I've come to realize just how much he means to me, and how much I mean to him.

When Travis left, I thought it was because I still had my baby weight. I just couldn't lose it. After he took Maddie, I had the opportunity to talk to him and ask him why he left. He told me what happened at that party and how it changed what we had. He was ashamed, but there was nothing he could do to change it. He admitted it was his fault and how what he did was the cowardly way out. But I did confirm that if I had found out, I would've left him anyway. That is the one thing I always knew I wouldn't deal with —cheating. Even if I haven't always had the best self-esteem, I know that I'm worth more than being cheated on. I feel like I finally have closure. But I also know there's a price on his head. He might not make it out of prison alive. Part of me is a little sad, but another part says he dug his own grave. He took my daughter and put her in a situation where she could've died. There's no forgiving that.

I look into Hollis' baby blues and see he's sincere.

"Yes," I whisper as a tear falls.

He wraps his arms around me. "Is that a yes to both questions?"

I nod as I embrace him. He lets go of me to roll over to his nightstand and comes back with a ring. It's a perfect princess-cut diamond. He places it on my finger and then kisses it.

Today my baby—our baby, is starting at a new school. It's closer to where we live and it's definitely more secure than her last one. This one is aware of the MC and I know they'll follow through with their rules, not like her old school. I really thought they were secure there, but I found out the hard way they weren't.

I kiss Hollis one more time before I roll out of bed to grab a quick shower. Of course he follows me and my quick shower gets a little longer, but I'm not complaining. He constantly finds new ways to make me feel sexy and I love it.

After we get dressed, I head to the kitchen to make breakfast, and Hollis goes and wakes up our Maddie. Ours. I love it when he calls her his daughter. I know she's always wanted a daddy. I was afraid I would never be able to give her one, but now she has one in Hollis. In fact, the whole club has embraced her. She's become best friends with Saoirse Bastianini and I love watching their friendship grow. Saoirse is one year younger so she won't be the same class as Maddie. But she will be in the same school, because it's pre-K to eighth grade. Granchio is Saoirse's bodyguard and he's offered to be Maddie's too.

I smile as I see my loves come into the kitchen. I put their plates in front of them.

"Are you excited for your new school?" I ask Maddie.

She nods. "I get to see Saoirse there too."

I chuckle. "But you know that you won't be

in the same class, right? You might get to see each other at recess, though."

"That's okay, Mommy. We can play when we get home." She smiles, then frowns a little.

"What's wrong?" Hollis asks her.

"Can you be my daddy?" she asks him.

Hollis looks at Maddie, then at me. "We should tell her," he says.

I nod at him. "You can tell her."

The smile that spreads across his face is priceless.

"I asked your mommy to marry me. And I asked her if I could adopt you."

She tilts her head to the side and thinks. "Does that mean you'll be my daddy?"

"Yes, baby. I will be your daddy."

Maddie jumps off her chair and onto Hollis' lap. She wraps her arms around his neck. "Can I call you 'Daddy' now?"

He chuckles at her. "If that's what you want. Yes."

"Yay! I love you, Daddy. So the mean man's not my daddy anymore, is he?"

I don't know how to explain this part to Maddie. How do you tell your five year old that Travis is her biological father and always will be, but Hollis is her daddy? The one that will be there for her for the rest of her life? Sometimes being a parent is harder than it seems.

Hollis

"Maddie, Travis is your father. I'm your daddy. I know that's confusing for you, but one day you'll understand. All you need to know is that I'll be here for you from now on. No matter what," I explain to her. I'm not sure how much she really understands, but I know that I have the rest of our lives to prove to her the difference between a 'father' and a 'daddy'. I know firsthand that being a father does not mean you're a daddy.

Maddie hugs me tighter, and it makes me feel like a superhero. I will always protect my family. My chosen family.

Since it's Maddie and Saoirses' first day of

school, Francesco, Maeve, Granchio, Lila and I are taking them to school. Starting tomorrow, only Granchio will take them and stay with them all day, unless there's something important he needs to do for the club. I know he'll protect our girls and keep them safe.

Epilogue

Lila

It's been a year since the night I went home with Hollis. And what a year it's been. Travis is still in jail. He's asked to talk to me but I said no. I learned everything I needed to the day he was caught. I remember the pain I was in when he abandoned us, but now I'm glad he did. If he hadn't, I never would've met Hollis. Or if I did, I never would've gone home with him. And my life wouldn't be what it is today.

Maddie has changed so much this last year. She was always a happy kid. After Travis and Shawna took her, she shut down for a while. But lately she's started talking about how scared she was when it happened. How even though Shawna told her I didn't want her, she knew that was a lie. She said she kept telling herself that Hollis and I would come and rescue her. She also told us Shawna hit her because she wouldn't listen to her. It happened more than once in the ten hours they had her.

I wish I had been able to get my hands on her. But at the same time, I'm glad she's dead. We never have to worry about her coming after our baby again. That kind of closure is what has helped all of us heal.

We got married a month ago, which Charmy won't stop teasing me about. She and Liam still aren't married, but they will be next month. Hollis didn't want to wait for them to get married first. Okay, *we* didn't want to wait.

My husband. Sometimes I find myself just staring at him, wondering how I got so lucky for him to have chosen me. There's been some new bunnies at the clubhouse and they've learned real fast that they can't put their hands on him. Some have made comments about me and my physique. They got banned pretty quick, and the other bunnies are learning to keep their hands off my man and their mouths shut.

Hollis

My wife. She thinks she's the lucky one in this marriage. But she's wrong. That title goes to me. My cupcake is the most beautiful woman inside and out. She's not only become my wife, but she's given me a family. I thought I had everything I needed. Then I met her, and Maddie. Now that we're married, I spend my time bugging her to have more babies. I mean, Maddie is six now and I think it's time to give her some siblings.

"Morning, cupcake."

"Morning, my love."

I wrap my arms around her. "What are you doing today?"

"Well, I have a doctor's appointment at nine-thirty."

I frown. "Is something wrong? Are you okay?"

"I'm fine. Would you like to come with me?"

"Of course I want to come. Are you sure you're okay?" I ask again. This is the first time she's mentioned an appointment.

"I promise, I'm okay. It's just a regular visit."

There's something in Lila's voice that I just can't put my finger on. It sounds like she's keeping something from me. And I don't like it.

"We should get up and get breakfast going," she says as she stretches.

I squint at her and she starts to giggle. Now I know she's keeping something from me. But I'll play along for now.

After we eat breakfast and send Maddie off to school with Granchio, we both get dressed for her appointment.

"Do you want to take my bike? Or the cage?" I ask her.

"I'd like to ride the bike today. One day I might not be able to ride with you."

Wait, what? Why wouldn't she be able to ride with me? I don't know what to say, so I frown at her more.

"Stop frowning at me, Hollis. I know you're trying to figure out if something is wrong with me. Nothing's wrong. I promise."

I continue to frown at her as we finish getting ready. Lila puts an address into the map on my phone and we're off. I follow where it tells me to go.

When we get to the doctor's office, I stand with Lila as she checks in. They say it's going to just be a few minutes, so we go and sit down in the waiting room. Finally after what feels like years, they call Lila's name. They show us to a room and tell me to wait there while they take her to get her vitals and whatever else they do back there. I look around the room and see lots of baby stuff on the walls. Lila comes back in and sits on the table.

"They said the doctor will be with us in a few minutes," she says.

"What's the appointment for?" I ask her.

"You'll see." She gives me a smile.

Again it feels like we've been waiting for a really long time. There's a knock at the door and it opens.

"Hi, I'm April, the ultrasound tech. You must be Lila and Hollis. It's nice to meet you both," she says as she shakes our hands. "Okay, Lila, I'm going to have you lay back and I'll get the machine up and running."

What in the fuck is going on? Ultrasound? Is Lila sick? Now I'm panicking and I don't know what to do. I watch April squirt some weird stuff that looks like lube on Lila's belly. All of a sudden there's a thumping sound. Holy fuck.

"Is that—?" I start to say as Lila softly chuckles.

"That's your baby's heartbeat," April says. "See that? There's your baby."

I stare at the screen. I see this tiny thing that looks like a gummy bear. I kiss Lila.

"Baby," I say as I sniffle. Grown men don't cry, right? Wrong. When you see your gummy bear for the first time, you cry.

"I'll grab some screenshots and then you can clean up. Doctor Matthews will be in to talk to you soon." April smiles at us. "Congratulations."

We each thank her as I take the pictures from her.

"How long have you known?" I ask Lila.

"I didn't really know till last week. I took a home test, but I wanted to be sure. And since I had a few complications with Maddie, I asked for an ultrasound. I wanted to surprise you."

I kiss her with everything I have. "I love you so fucking much, cupcake. So fucking much."

There's a knock at the door again. "Hi, I'm Doctor Matthews. You must be Lila and Hollis," he says as he shakes both our hands. He sits down and faces us.

"Your baby looks healthy, and by the measurements, you're about three months along. We can do another ultrasound in a month if you'd like to know the sex. If you don't, then I would like to see you for a check-up anyway. And then you'll have another ultrasound at six months," he says to us.

"We aren't sure if we want to know." Lila chuckles. "We haven't discussed anything just yet."

"No problem. You can call the office and make the appointment or make one today and cancel if you need to. Congratulations Mom and Dad," he smiles at us and shakes our hands again before leaving.

"Are you okay, Hollis?"

I nod. "I'm more than okay. We're having a baby—Maddie's gonna be a big sister."

Lila's smiling at me as she gets off the table.

"Thank you, my love. For everything you've given me," I say as I kiss her again.

"You've given me everything I've ever wanted. I can't wait to meet our baby."

Hi! I'm Natalie. I published my first book, Aftermath in August 2021. I've been lucky enough to find my own insta-love-at-first-sight person. We have a daughter who drives us crazy and a corgi who adds to the chaos. I love hockey (Chicago Blackhawks), MotoGP (Motorcycle Racing), and baseball (Chicago Cubs). When I'm not writing, you can find me studying or crafting. Or crafting when I should be studying.

Nataliearthurbooks.com

Giovanna

Everything I thought about my life was a lie and
because of that, trust became non-existent for me.
Then I met Declan. He pushed his way into my life,
determined to prove to me that not everyone is a liar.
He's a hockey player and we all know the reputation of

hockey players. But I want to trust someone again…
maybe he's the one?

<u>Declan</u>

Hockey has been my focus for as long as I can remember. The day I met Giovanna, my life changed. Hockey would always be my first love. But she would be my last. Something happened to her and she's afraid to trust me. But that's okay, I'll show her that I'm real. That we're real.

Aftermath is the first book in my Mancini Legacy Series. All books are standalone, but it's best if read in order. There is mention of characters from my Cimaruta MC Chicago Series.

https://books2read.com/Aftermath-ManciniLegacy

Sebastiano

I had given up on meeting my person, content to be the protector of my family. Then one day I met her. But someone else was laying claim to her. If she was happy, I would step back and watch her from afar. But then I saw the marks on her and I knew I needed to save her.

Schuyler

It seems like I've been struggling most of my life. Just my sister and me against the world. Then I thought I met the man of my dreams. Turns out he's the man from my nightmares. I can't run and I can't escape from him. Then I met Sebastiano. He made me feel safe from the moment he took my hand in his. He says I will be his, but he doesn't know about the monster that's in my life. The one that won't let go.

Saving Her is the second book in my Mancini Legacy Series. All books are standalone, but it's best if read in order. There is mention of characters from my Cimaruta MC Chicago Series.

https://books2read.com/SavingHer-ManciniLegacy

Luciana

Women on an MC council? It's unheard of until now. Love at first sight? That's a new one for me too. I was convinced I didn't need someone to make me happy.

Then I slammed into Rónán.

Literally.

In an instant, he turned my world upside down. But can he handle the MC life?

Rónán

My life was going the way I planned it. Then the most beautiful woman stepped into my path and changed my life forever. I know she's keeping things from me. And that's okay...for now.

Because she's mine.

She just doesn't know it yet.

Choices is the first book in my Cimaruta MC Chicago Series. All books are standalone, but it's best if read in order. There is mention of characters from my Mancini Legacy Series.

https://books2read.com/Choices-CimarutaMCChicago

Francesco

I met the love of my life at fourteen. She had my heart the moment I saw her. But when you're young and stupid you don't always make the right decisions. That's what happened to me. I let the temptations of my job distract me from the one thing I couldn't live without. I had lost all hope, but fate gave me another chance. I have to make it up to her. I know she's hiding something from me. Will she let me in and give me a second chance?

<u>**Maeve**</u>

I thought I had it all. Sure I may have been young, but when it's real, you just know. That was, until he ended things. I never saw it coming. Now he's back and he wants another chance. Can I really trust him not to break my heart again? I want to believe him. I've never stopped loving him. But it's not just me I have to protect anymore.

Can they find their way back to the happily ever after they were meant to have? Or will they be pulled apart again, shattering all hope?

Reclaiming Our Forever is the second book in my Cimaruta MC Chicago Series. All books are standalone, but it's best if read in order. There is mention of characters from my Mancini Legacy Series.

https://books2read.com/ReclaimingOurForever-CimarutaMCChicago

<u>Amante</u>

Relationship? No.

Love? Hell no.

Forever? Never.

A quick hook up and that was that. I had my family and my club and that's all I needed. Until the day she walked in. With her I wanted more than one night, but when I got out of the shower she was gone. But I will find her. Then I'll just have to convince her we belong together.

<u>Charmaine</u>

Love is nothing but a lie. I watched my parents crash and burn and nothing and no one could change my mind. Until him. My tattooed, hunky biker man. Wait, did I say mine? That can't happen. But he says all the right things, and makes me feel like I'm the most special girl in the world. Can we make it work?

Notch the Plan is part of the Notchin' Boots Series. There is mention of characters from my Mancini Legacy Series and my Cimaruta MC Chicago Series.

https://books2read.com/NotchThePlan-NotchinBoots

Kostas

Mating matches keep the peace in our world. So why did it feel like my life was over when it was my turn? She hated me from the moment we were paired. And to be honest? I hated her too. So when she rejected me for some loser from another clan, it didn't bother me that much. But then I met her—the one the fates chose for me—and everything just felt right. I knew in an instant that she was the one I would never let go of.

Artemis

In our world, mates can be either fated or chosen, but

finding your fated mate is never guaranteed. I thought I had chosen someone who could love me and we would spend our lives together. But then he rejected me—for my BEST FRIEND. That day, I decided I was fine being alone. But then, completely by chance, I met someone who felt like home. Could this really be it? The forever I secretly craved...my fated one.

My Fated One is part of the Fated Mates Series. There is mention of characters from my Mancini Legacy Series and my Cimaruta MC Chicago Series.

https://books2read.com/MyFatedOne-FatedMates

<u>Aiden</u>

Motorcycle racing has been my life since I could walk
and talk. It was all I ever needed. Or so I thought.
Then I met the one woman that made me want more.
One day, the unthinkable happens—a racing accident
causes me to lose all my memories of her. But I still feel
her in my soul, even if my brain can't remember her.

<u>Élodie</u>

I wanted a knight in shining armor, but what I got was
a wolf in disguise. After escaping from him, I met a
man willing to give me everything I ever wanted. Then

in a split second, he was taken from me. Not physically, but mentally. The man I love doesn't remember who I am, but I'm determined to get him back.

Racing Back to Love is part of the Forget-Me-Not Series. There is mention of characters from my Mancini Legacy Series.

https://books2read.com/RacingBackToLove-ForgetMeNot

www.ingramcontent.com/pod-product-compliance
Lightning Source LLC
Chambersburg PA
CBHW061539310726
48972CB00008B/2523